CROWN OF CARRION

By Jeremy Megargee

Crown of Carrion by Jeremy Megargee

© 2024, Jeremy Megargee

All rights reserved.

Published in the United States by
Curious Corvid Publishing, LLC, Ohio.

No part of this publication may be reproduced, stored in a retrieval system,
stored in a database and / or published in any form or by any means, electronic,
mechanical, photocopying, recording or otherwise, without the prior written
permission of the publisher, except as permitted by U.S. copyright law.

Cover Art by Mitch Green, Rad Press Studios
Formatting by Ravven White

ISBN: 978-1-959860-40-2

Printed in the United States of America

Curious Corvid Publishing, LLC

PO Box 204

Geneva, OH 44041

This is a work of fiction. Unless otherwise indicated, all the names, characters,
businesses, places, events and incidents in this book are either the product of the
author's imagination or used in a fictitious manner. Any resemblance to actual
persons, living or dead, or actual events is purely coincidental.

www.curiouscorvidpublishing.com

First Edition

DEDICATION

For those with hearts that cannot help but howl...

Carnies are a different breed. Fingers stained with nicotine, skin baked red and raw by harsh parking lot sunbeams, voices just guttural entreaties designed to draw the rubes in and make them open their wallets and spill out the contents for the taking. They're a traveling subspecies of humanity. Merely rusted-out rides erected in Walmart parking lots, most of them prehistoric, but that doesn't stop people from coming and slapping their tickets into dirty hands for the chance to spin their troubles away. The stench of popcorn and funnel cake mingles with warm vomit from an overzealous child who chanced the carousel after filling up on sweets, and sawdust is poured down on that pool of undigested slop like it's the most commonplace occurrence in the world. And for the carnies, maybe it is.

Merrill sniffs the air, tasting this atmosphere of distraction and deception, seeing all the glimmering bulbs painting the faces of thieves that hide in plain sight under stretches of canopy tent.

He's not here for entertainment. No children follow at his ankles, and no warmth exists in his face. He's an outsider even in this mecca of outsiders, and for him that's the norm, and it's always suited Merrill just fine. He's hunting, and his quarry isn't far. The colorful tents whip in the heat of the day, and when Merrill enters through the threshold of one, the temperature inside is almost stifling. It's a sauna, and the discomfort causes a rumble to begin low in his throat. He swallows it down as best he can, craning his neck and side-eyeing the dim confines of this little round room.

"Seeking a fortune, traveler?"

She's old now. Hair braided up into white dreads, a sad gray cataract eating up one eye, jowls that ripple slightly as she shifts in her chair. It's hard to judge her weight, but it seems like her robes swallow her, the material tattered and long unwashed, so many forgotten stars and crescent moons in a universe that lacks a future.

Merrill grunts and looks down at the small chair across from her. He wears jeans covered in road dust, a black dress shirt tucked in, and a sheepskin jacket overtop the shirt. His hair is wild, long, a tangled mane, and his facial features are difficult to describe. Rugged. A face like a hatchet that has been splitting firewood for a long time. Ruddy cheek flesh on sharp cheekbones, lips thin, irises blacker than pitch. They don't seem like a man's eyes. They're more akin to a shark in the shallows, waiting for that perfect chance to dart forth and nibble.

"Where's your crystal ball? Or are we throwing chicken bones across the table. . ."

She chuckles a dry chain-smoker's laugh, and he's concerned it might turn into a cough that she won't be able to stop, but she reins it in at the last moment.

"In this tent, we do it the old way. No baubles or props. I just need a palm. Everything I'm meant to see will be written there."

"And what of the things you're not meant to see?"

"They'll be there too. Divination offers up no dark crannies to hide things in your heart. It all comes out, one way or another. . ."

Merrill lowers himself into the seat. He's a big man, and it creaks under his burden. He leans forward, a toothpick shifting from the left side of his mouth to the right. There's a grin lurking somewhere behind that toothpick. It's playful, but not in a good way.

He pulls back the sleeve of his jacket, and he offers up a hand to the fortune teller.

"Mistress Martine gratefully accepts this palm, and just so we're clear, it'll be cash or credit when the reading is through."

The old woman allows her eyelids to flutter closed, and she starts to weave her fingertips across Merrill's palm, tracing the deep grooves that are etched in his flesh.

"These are rough hands. They've had blood on them. . ."

"They will again. Nature of the beast."

"What line of work are you in, Mister. . .?"

"Sade. Merrill Sade. And I suppose you could call me a collection agent. . ."

"A thankless job at times."

"Ah hell, someone's gotta do it, right?"

There's an element of theater in Merrill. It's like he knows this is a performance, and he's having too much fun to leave the stage.

"I'm getting that you're an animal lover. I see forests with ancient trees. I see deer. I see teeth that gnash in the night. . ."

"You see much, old woman. But do you see deeper?"

The slightest tremor passes through her fingers. She tries to conceal it, but Merrill notices. There isn't much that he doesn't notice.

"Saliva. Paw prints in soil. Bark that's been torn and marked. There's a glow in the heavens, a terrible lamplight glow in the midnight hours, and it lords over you. I'm smelling things, too. Smells like wet dog, Mister Sade. Do you have a dog?"

"Not quite. I think a dog is a tragic creature. So domesticated. So neutered and apart from its instincts. A family dog is prone to snap, and when a chunk of meat is taken out of a beloved toddler trying to cuddle that family dog, I think the family should blame themselves. Because they put their trust in an animal. It's unwise to trust an animal, Martine."

The old woman keeps her eyes closed, but if she were to open them now, she'd see that Merrill's smile has enlarged. It glistens in the candlelight of the tent, and deep in that throat corridor of his, a rumble is born anew.

"I see meat. Gore. I see skin opening and veins ripping and blood coating a liar's tongue, and I wish to see no more. Why have you come here, Mister Sade?"

Now it's Merrill's turn to laugh. His eyes twinkle, and there's something hyena-like about his glare.

"Aren't you the fortune teller? Tell me what happens next."

He watches the loose skin of her neck as she swallows. He feels her try to pull her hand free, but his grip hardens, and the bones of her wrist feel as weak as those of a baby bird's still in the nest.

The rumble in Merrill's throat becomes a percussive growl, and as he stands, his face spirals out to become a snout, and the canines grow like railroad spikes, and his hot, eager tongue lashes from side to side behind them. Mistress Martine is baptized in slobber, and before she can breathe in deeply enough to summon a scream, she is being torn. She's frail, and it doesn't take much.

Merrill rag-dolls her across that little tent, biting and raking the flesh from her bones, and when she's trying to crawl away, with her spine jutting up from her skin like a crooked broomstick, he eases a boot down between her shoulder blades, the tips of his claws just beginning to pierce the leather, and he doesn't let up until he hears the satisfying snap of vertebrae.

"I tried to tell you before—"

His voice is jagged music, the vocal cords warped, and he kneels over her corpse to gather up something that was near and dear to her.

"—I've come to collect."

The valley is tucked away in the Appalachian Mountains, a region largely untouched by time. It's a sea of green trees with hollers and backroads, and the homestead is far above any town or pocket of civilization. That's exactly how Ivy and her kin like it. Virgin land to call their own, and a sense of removal from society as a whole.

The cabins and outbuildings are stretched all across the open hillside, and roosters and chickens roam freely, horses are corralled in a barn, and there's so much viable garden space for fresh vegetables of all shapes and sizes to be grown on the property. Her people operate with limited technology, but they aren't complete Luddites, and enormous solar panels dominate the side of the hill that gets the most intense sunlight in the mornings.

It's a tight-knit familial setting, and there isn't a soul in the homestead that is unfamiliar. Everyone knows everyone, and everyone contributes. They're a territorial lot, and it's been decades since a stranger has sought them out or stumbled onto their land by accident. They're so deep in the unmapped wilderness that the old-growth hemlocks surrounding them act as a barrier to the outside world, even to the most adventurous hunter or hiker who might wander far out into the rustic backcountry.

Despite the isolation, Ivy has never felt alone. She was born and raised in the homestead. Her parents died when she was young, but her uncles, aunts, and old community elders had a hand in teaching her and helping her grow into the young woman that she is today. They taught her how to read, write, and, when that first change came with puberty, the elders even taught her how to wet her fangs and merge with the lupine gift that she carried in her DNA.

That's the most important aspect of the homestead. The reason for the isolation, exclusivity, and wariness of outsiders. Every man, woman, and child who calls this place home carries in them the wolf blood, and if there was ever a superpack for Ivy's kind, it's here in Merkel Valley.

The members of the superpack are known for living *clean* lives. There are wolves all over in pocket clans, most of them rogues and cutthroats who freely murder and feast on humans, but that isn't the way for Ivy's kin. When in lupine form, they hunt only the game that the forest provides, and when not hunting under the glow of Mother Moon, they live mostly in their human forms, cultivating the land, fostering families, and maintaining a level of peace that isn't often found in the cities far below. They worship Mother Moon, all of them religious, but that is something deeply ingrained in the biology of a wolf.

When Mother Moon opens up her fullness to them, the beams bring strength, and there is no greater lust in life than to run through the ferns, navigating ravines and clambering over rotting tree trunks, the scent of deer, rabbit, or even bear teasing at the nostrils and promising succulent meat. . .

When Ivy thinks of the great hunt, saliva bursts into her mouth, and she has to actively keep her eyes from glazing over. That's something else you learn growing up in Merkel Valley. The importance of control. How to befriend the beast inside of you, rein him or her in when necessary, and make of your life the perfect marriage of human and animal instincts.

That's something most lone wolves have to learn on their own, and she doesn't envy them that burden. The change can be incredibly jarring and traumatic, and without some level of guidance, it's like waking up and realizing that your body has turned against you. It drives wolves to dark places and unspeakable acts, and she's heard of cabals that form through that shared pain and animalistic hatred. . .

She's grateful that isn't the case here.

Her nimble fingers are busy planting mint and basil in the herb garden near her cabin, wavy locks of chestnut hair falling down against her freckled cheeks. She's sweating, but it's the good kind of sweat, born of a body in motion and hard labor that utilizes her bare hands.

She sees Braun approaching from near the compost heap—a big, barrel-chested man with a beard so wild you'd think that squirrels nest in it—and if there was ever someone in Merkel Valley that the other wolves looked to as their de facto leader, this is the man.

He's usually cheery and good-humored, but today his expression is dour. There are clouds in his eyes and his head seems heavy, struggling even to meet her gaze when he's within a few feet of where she crouches.

"There will be a tribunal tonight, Ivy. I thought it best you heard it from me first, before the rumor mill starts to churn."

She breathes in deeply through her nose, turning her eyes skyward. The sunlight settles into her pores, and with it, a sense of anxiety that overtakes the serenity. She wipes the dirt from her fingertips on her thighs, letting a sigh fall out from lips that carry the slightest tremble.

"Merrill?"

Braun shifts his girth, and that bearded head offers her a quick and curt nod.

"Merrill."

Ivy gazes deep into the massive bonfire, watching the cinders dance and the flames twisting higher. There's controlled chaos in the inferno, and it makes her think of Merrill. He has always been cagey, ever the opportunist. She can still recall a time from their shared youth when Merrill had some of the smaller kids hunting morel mushrooms for him in the hills, and when they'd gather them up into baskets, he'd sell them off around the homestead and give his pickers a percentage. An ambitious boy even then, and charismatic enough to gain a following.

The night music is loud all around them: crickets chirping, toads singing, and owls hooting from high places. The coyotes are yipping to each other somewhere on the western ridge, and on this night, Ivy wishes she were among them. She'd rather be a cricket, a toad, a coyote, anything but a wolf with atrocities to dwell on. Atrocities committed by someone she once loved, no less. But that was years ago. That was another life. . .

Almost every member of the community is gathered around the bonfire, with the exception of the children. The little ones were put to bed early tonight so this business could be addressed. There are so many familiar faces painted in the warm glow of the firelight, most of them standing, and some sitting on carved oaken chairs closer to the stone circle surrounding the fire pit. There's old Matilda with her hair spun up into a ball on her head, looking like gray spider silk. There's Abel with his spectacles, quiet Abel, thoughtful Abel, almost a historian for Merkel Valley and the generations that the homestead has fostered. And in the center, with a ceremonial staff in his hand, Braun stands tall. There's a black bear pelt slung across his shoulder, and he's slicked his beard down with grooming oil tonight, doing his best to appear respectable in front of his people.

"Some of the elders among us might remember Martine. She came from a family of traveling gypsies, and they'd often trade with our grandparents up here decades ago. She never knew our true nature, but I've often thought that she suspected. That was before we tightened the borders to strangers. It was a safer world then. . ."

Braun rubs his staff in the ash of the fire, stirring it up, and the embers show their agitation by burning even redder.

"She was murdered in Virginia yesterday. She'd been working for a little parking lot carnival, and the artifact that was entrusted to her was taken. We got the word late from our connections below, and from what I was told, her flesh was shredded into ribbons. There can be no mistake. This slaughter was carried out by a rogue wolf—"

Murmurs and groans from the crowd, and when Matilda chimes in, her voice is so soft and wispy that the others have to lean closer in order to hear her.

"Martine had a good heart. It was a wild heart, much like what beats in our own chests, but a good one. She didn't deserve this."

A booming voice from the back of the crowd, and Ivy can't quite make out the speaker. Perhaps either Pyke or Duke, the two blacksmiths in Merkel Valley.

"It's a farce to sit here and pretend like we don't know the facts. This was the poison that was purged from our own kindred. Even when banished, he still finds a way to bring shame to our species."

Braun raises the staff, shaking the timber rattlesnake tails on the knob at the top to reestablish order.

"I'll not waste words on speculation. It was Merrill. His scent was smeared across the old woman's body, and he made no attempt to conceal it. It's been years since he was excommunicated, but it seems he's been busy in his wanderings. He's made his den in the cities below, and I fear that cutting him off from us has only made his proclivities worse."

That loud voice again, and this time Ivy is able to make out the face: Duke, stepping forward with his hands on his hips, ample gut hanging over his belt.

"His queer ideas are what undid him here. Always raving about some wolfen god and reading that tainted scripture. He's full of delusions. And I know I'm not the only one to hear this, but there are rumors that he has men and women working with him below. Mortals that consume the flesh of their own to gain his favor in hopes of one day being made into wolves themselves. I think Merrill was born mad, but to have cannibals doing his dirty work? Imagine the perversion of that, the obscenity of his hubris. . ."

Ivy has held her silence for as long as she can, and it's finally time for her to break it.

"He wasn't born mad, Duke. People here conveniently forget that there was good in him once. What he's done is unforgivable, but he was not always like this."

"With respect, Ivy, you were his lover once, and there will always be a part of you that sympathizes with him. But we cannot allow this transgression. If we ignore this, he will not stop. Those artifacts mean more than food and water to him. His obsession has deep roots—"

Braun clamps a hand onto Duke's shoulder and gently pulls him back from the fire, and the blacksmith reluctantly bows his head and swallows whatever words he has left to say.

"I understand how upsetting this is to all of you. I understand that many of us had friendships and ties to Merrill in the past, but he allowed those to shatter with his own actions. He does not pray to Mother Moon. His beliefs are far darker and stranger, but they are his own."

Braun's gaze hardens, and he scans the faces of his kin, seeing the pain and confusion that have festered in them since this news broke.

"We must decide how to address this. It's against our creed to let him rampage unchecked. He must answer for his lack of control. I intend to send a small group after his scent, and when he is found. . ."

Braun pauses, and before he can continue, Ivy leaps to her feet, passion making her cheeks blush like roses.

"Let me go, Braun. I can reason with him. I can remind him of what he used to be before his path forked into blacker, deader trees. There has to be something left of that boy I knew, even if it's nothing but a scrap. . ."

She feels tears in her eyes, but she doesn't let them spill. Her jaw tightens, and she pulls strength from the animal within.

"And if there is no hope, I promise you, I will extract his heart myself."

A wave of silence passes through the crowd, no sound to be heard but the crackling of the fire. Ivy is almost certain this request will be denied, but Braun surprises her.

"Very well, Ivy. We'll put our trust into you, but you'll not hunt him alone. You'll take two of our finest, and you'll choose them yourself. But I warn you now, if he'll not turn from this path, I want his canines pulled from his gums and brought to me. Am I understood?"

"Yes, Braun. You have my word."

"Sleep on your decision tonight, and you'll choose your companions at first light. Once that's done, you'll go, and for the good of the pack, you'll do what needs doing."

He speaks no more, and soon her people start to drift off from the tribunal bonfire, and before Ivy even realizes it, she's sitting there alone, watching its life slowly fade as the heat dies and the embers blacken.

Was it wise to volunteer, or has she damned herself?

Ivy slept fitfully and awoke with dawn, but during her tossing and turning, decisions were finalized. She knows who she wants, and she sets out to gain her companions. Pyke is up early too, the more humorous and good-hearted of the blacksmith pair, a great opposite to Duke's opinionated harshness. She finds him fashioning a pitchfork near the back of his workshop, and the moment she approaches, he crosses those big arms and offers her a trademark smirk.

Pyke is a burly behemoth of a man: head shaved bald and scarred rivets decorating one cheek from his battle with a rabid alpha many decades past. People used to say Merrill was big at six foot three and over two hundred pounds, but Pyke makes him seem small in comparison, standing in at six foot eight and just a little over the three-hundred-pound mark.

"Word is you're playing recruiter today, Ivy."

"I might just be. Can't say I've had too many volunteers running to join up. . ."

Pyke scoffs, his smirk growing into a full-fledged smile.

"Yellowbellies, the lot of them. They'd rather hunt rabbits and gophers than leave their precious utopia. I love it here too, but a sense of adventure makes life taste all the better, don't you think?"

"That's why I'm coming to you first, Pyke. You know the risk, and you know Merrill. With all that in mind, I could use a hunter like you. A *wolf* like you."

"Don't you make me blush red like a schoolgirl out here, little lady."

His eyes fall to the earth, and some of the playfulness leaves his voice.

"Aye, I know Merrill. I know the bastard is off the rails. And honestly, Ivy? It would give me great pleasure to knock some sense into him. Make him remember his roots a bit. So if you're asking me to come with you, then it won't take much convincing."

He bows like a muscle-bound high school theater kid, and gently places the pitchfork into Ivy's hands.

"You have my pitchfork."

Ivy snorts laughter and tosses the handle back to him.

"I don't think we'll be raking up cow manure where we're going, so you can leave that here, but I'll certainly take you. Seriously, Pyke. It means a lot that you'll come."

She reaches out and damn near has to stand on her tippy-toes to plant a hand on his shoulder, but he covers it with his own calloused fingers.

"So, any other ideas on who else you want to be in our little ragtag group of lycanthropic saviors?"

"I was thinking Abel."

"Hm. An interesting choice. Abel is more at home with his books and his quill pen, though I'll never fault the man for his love of learning. But if things get bad, I can't imagine him in a fight."

"Hopefully it won't come to that. But I feel we need him. His knowledge is pivotal. Most people think Merrill's ideologies are just the ravings of a despot, but we both know there's more to it. That deity that Merrill clings to. . ."

"Abel knows about it. He knows how damaging it would be to not just Merkel Valley, but all the wolves that roam this world. Someone with his intellect might just turn the tide in our favor."

"Consider me sold then."

"Maybe we approach him together? Two against one?"

"Let's do it. You're good cop, I'm bad cop. I'll give him a motivational noogie to join the cause."

Ivy and Pyke start off in the direction of the community's own little Historical Society building, the sun still rising in the sky. They keep the mood lighthearted because they know that what awaits them is anything but that.

Abel rests his hands on a stack of leather-bound tomes, and his gaze flits back and forth between Pyke and Ivy. They're in his study, a room that smells of old books and spilled ink, bookcases reaching high to the circular ceiling with rolling ladders on both sides.

"I'm not opposed to going, but do you think I'll be of much use to you on the road? I'm comfortable with these—"

He motions to the books that dominate the room.

"—but modern human beings are another story."

Ivy smiles, liking his blunt honesty.

"You're the man I want, Abel. I know you had no control over the rabbit hole he fell down, but Merrill would come here and read when he was younger. It's where it all started for him."

Abel takes a moment to respond, his neck craning so that he can look out the window. Sunlight hits the lenses of his glasses, reflecting a warm, canary-yellow glow.

"*Apollo Lykaios*. I wish I had done more then. I encouraged his reading. I thought it was a beautiful thing that Merrill wanted to learn more about the history of our species. I could have stopped him from getting lost in those moth-eaten pages, but I didn't. I'll carry that guilt for the rest of my days."

Ivy struggles to find the words to respond, and she simply goes to the man and slings an arm across his shoulders.

"You couldn't have known. None of us could have known. If you give a boy a matchstick, you're teaching him to warm himself with fire. You don't expect that he'll become enchanted by the conflagration. That he'll dive headfirst into his own inferno."

Pyke is picking up a few books on the table and looking at the titles, but it's clear that he's a fish out of water in Abel's world.

"Abel, I've always been hazy on the details. Tell me about Apollo Lykaios. And remember that you're explaining it to a big dumb son of a bitch, alright?"

"You know our religion, Pyke. We are children of the moon, and the moon is what we worship. Our goddess. She who brings the change. Mother Moon. But there is another god. His lore is coated in dust, his fangs dull, and his name all but forgotten even among the oldest pureborn wolves. Apollo Lykaios. The Greeks prayed to him in the ancient days, even erected temples to gain his favor. The old wolf god. Lord of the Wilderness, paw prints like craters in the earth, and a hunger so insatiable that his tongue always lolled, and when his saliva hit the soil, rivers were born of it. . ."

A silence descends on the study. There's a light wind outside, and all three wolves notice. Their senses are heightened, and the resurrection of the old god's name causes goosebumps to rise on their skin.

"There was a festival that honored him in rustic Arcadia. It took place on Mount Lykaion, their tallest peak. Great tables out in the open, feasts of meat, fruit, and women. Carnality. Perverse rites. Human sacrifice. And the lynchpin of the festival—the act of cannibalism. The consumption of human flesh under starlight. It was all meant to be a showcase, a sort of summoning. Drawing Apollo Lykaios into the fabric of our reality to sup on blood everlasting."

Pyke leans back, suddenly claustrophobic in the small study. The big man is keenly aware of how the walls seem to press down on him. . .

"Just stories, right? Myth and legend."

"Not to Merrill. He became enamored with the concept that Apollo Lykaios could be invoked, and that the right lycanthrope host would be able to sustain his essence. That's why he associates with cannibals and gathers them to his heel. That's why he hunts those *artifacts* like a wolf possessed. They are broken pieces of a lost crown carved of stone, and all the pieces must be found for him to complete the ritual. And believe me, he is not simply a mindless killing machine down there in the cities. He knows exactly what his aim is."

Ivy has heard most of this madness from Merrill's own mouth, but some of it still seems incomprehensible to her.

"If he were to find all the pieces, what then, Abel? Does he plan to travel to this mountain in Arcadia?"

"No. He believes Mount Lykaion can be more of a mental construct. An idea. The original setting doesn't matter, only the ritual itself. If memory serves, he told me he would find a suitable peak in the Appalachians, and he'd make of that his modern Mount Lykaion."

Pyke heaves a sigh and has to hunch his head down to move past a section of ceiling.

"Thanks for the lesson, professor. Sounds utterly batshit, but I appreciate it. Considering what we know, are we all still looking to track him down and do what Braun asked us to do?"

Abel wets his lips, and Ivy can tell it takes great will for him to answer.

"I'll always feel a level of responsibility for what Merrill became. I'll go. If we can right a wrong, I'm all for it."

Ivy nods, and she looks to both men. A warrior and a scholar. But more importantly, blood brothers. Pack mates. Her kin. She hopes sincerely that the bond they share will curry favor from Mother Moon on the journey ahead.

"We can't waste time. We have no idea how many of these artifacts Merrill has in his possession. He's proven that he has no problem murdering to get them. We'll need to pack light, and then we hunt."

"Any idea where we start, Ivy?"

"I've still got his scent. I've wished often that it would leave me, but it never has. A part of me thinks that he wants it to remain curled up in my nostrils. He's gone west. He and his acolytes. I smell the cacti and the drought."

Her nostrils expand, eyelids flutter closed.

"I smell the desert."

Ivy felt a surge of emotion swelling in her as they made their preparations to depart Merkel Valley. The place has always seemed like a womb to her, warm and familiar, and to venture out of it is always risky for their kind. She's been out on several scouting missions with other members of the superpack, usually trips to local grocers, farms, and even the cities for supply runs and to trade goods, but this would be different.

She's never been out to the western badlands. Even though the smell of the Mojave is in her nose, she's never set her eyes upon that landscape. It's totally alien to her, as barren as Merkel is plentiful. Pyke has ventured out much farther than her, so he has more experience with the world beyond the homestead. Abel has never once left the grounds, so she knows in her heart that this will be a major culture shock for him. She just hopes that he'll be able to adapt.

She kissed her great aunt's forehead before leaving the cabin, that old gray wolf looking up at her with watery eyes. Her aunt has always been a woman of few words, but their bond is a tight one. She made her promise that she'd take care of herself, and she made her promise that she'd bite first before allowing herself to be bitten. An old adage among the lycanthropes of the valley. Bite first before being bitten. . .

They stand now on the border of their territory, the tree line below separating them from the home that has always been etched into their identities. Braun stands before them with a gathering of their people watching from some distance behind.

"The weight of this is not lost on me. All three of you are strong, and although the path ahead is treacherous, I know Merkel Valley is being well represented."

He looks like a Goliath there on the hill, the incline forcing Ivy, Abel, and Pyke to all look up at Braun.

"Remember. If you cannot turn Merrill from his machinations, then defang him and snuff out the beast. There's nothing else we can do to ensure peace and to keep him from further bloodshed. And when it comes to his minions? Those cannibals—"

The slightest snarl crosses Braun's lips.

"—Make meals of them if you must. Smite them and show them the meaning of true hunger. Their numbers are great, but their flesh is frail. You have my permission to pick your teeth with their bones."

Nothing is left to be said. Ivy nods to Braun and the rest of the wolves behind him, and then she takes up her trekking pole and tightens the backpack on her shoulders. She leads her blood brothers into the mouth of the forest, and it swallows them up.

It feels real after the first few steps.

Leaving her ancestral home. Hunting Merrill. Miles and miles to go, and she hopes her will won't falter.

CHAPTER 6

Merrill walks through the encampment, breathing deeply of the sagebrush. Joshua trees provide little shade from the merciless Mojave sun, and battered RVs and rusting jalopies are parked all around in a huge circle on the desert hardpan. His people travel in a caravan, nomadic marauders that go where his preternatural nose tells them to go. He sees them lurking here and there, watching with devoted subservience as he passes. Street people, junkies, and wretched misfits from all corners of the country. He only has one rule for them. One commandment to follow in order to travel under the protection of a lycanthrope.

Eat your own.

Consume the flesh of your fellow man, and prove to Merrill that you have the makings of a wolf. It has become religion to them. They view him as a Christlike figure beyond the limits of frail mortality, and their conversion to cannibalism took no great convincing. The Great Promise looms on the horizon for his most loyal followers. When it is time to climb Mount Lykaion and perform the ritual, they'll be granted that long-awaited turn. He'll pierce them with tooth and claw, and he'll slop the lupine blood into their eager mouths. When he is a god, he'll birth his animalistic angels.

The camp has been set up in an abandoned rail yard, one of the few signs of civilization out in these badlands. They're probably about sixty miles from Las Vegas, and Merrill has made himself a temporary den in the last surviving boxcar. The wood is crumbling, and the interior has an almost fetid stench, but he likes that just fine. The worst odors are the best odors.

They stink of life and death and rot, and when the circle has closed, life again.

He sees a little campfire set up near the front of the boxcar. Several of his cannibals crouch around it. They're in the process of spit-roasting a human thigh, tearing off blackened meat with grubby fingers and relishing the flavor. They are scavengers, the lot of them. The wolves he was born with know that he associates with such lowly creatures, and they think him mad for it. But they don't understand. Scavengers have their purpose in the food chain. And their connection to a higher authority leads to food in their bellies, so it's beneficial to him too. The wolves look down on them because they're weak. It's easy for a single wolf to rip several human beings apart. But when the numbers game is on their side, it's different. His cannibals have been taught to know no fear. They care nothing for their own individual lives. All that they do is for the good of the clan. They're not wolves, like him, but Coyotes.

His loyal Coyotes.

Of the Coyotes, there are none more loyal than Harvey Hollow. He rises now from the campfire, a hunk of viscera in his balled fist. He chews as he approaches Merrill, his mouth opening up in a smile to display dark-smeared tombstone teeth. He's tall and thin, bald with a large forehead, and he's always wearing mirrored aviator sunglasses, even late into the night. Merrill can't even remember what color the man's eyes are because they're always hidden behind those lenses.

His limbs are etched and crisscrossed in self-harm scars from decades of mutilation. His olive skin is like a roadmap, and the first and last time Merrill asked him about those scars, Harvey told him that he'd been trying to "cut the demons out" for most of his life.

Merrill met Harvey in the old days when he was still fresh from his banishment from Merkel Valley. Harvey Hollow was his first soldier, and he found him living in a sewer tunnel in some little backwater town in New Mexico. When the two met, it was almost like fate predicting a legacy of violence. Now Harvey is his most trusted acolyte. His second in command. The man at the top of the Coyote hierarchy, and Merrill greets him in kind.

"Who's for dinner?"

"You wouldn't know her. Hungry, lobo?"

"Always."

Merrill takes the hunk of charred meat that Harvey Hollow offers him, and the two men begin to stroll around the border of the encampment.

"Did the gypsy have it?"

Merrill pulls a black, silken handkerchief from his jacket's inner pocket, and he shows Harvey the piece of archaic crown. It looks almost like a mixture of basalt and granite, but Merrill knows that even if geologists were able to study the stone, they wouldn't be able to determine its origins. He lets Harvey run his fingers over the texture. A mania seems to settle into his facial features, mouth twitching with vicious joy. . .

"It's warm. When I touch it, it's almost like there's a heartbeat. But not from a person, or even an animal. It's like the heartbeat of the forest. Every wilderness that ever was or will ever be. . ."

"It thirsts, Harvey Hollow. Each time the pieces are reunited with each other, the crown remembers what it used to be. It longs for the iron scent of blood, the rawness of meat chewed between teeth the size of redwoods. That time will come again. Apollo Lykaios will come again."

"Hallowed be thy name."

Merrill turns, lightly patting a hand across Harvey's pitted cheek. The cannibal mewls like an obedient kitten, pressing Sade's big hand closer to his skin.

"Remember what I've told you of my ancestral home? The betrayers. Those fearful moon-worshipers that close off their minds. There's still one I'm scent-bonded to. She's traveling beyond the limits of that valley, and I believe she intends to find me."

"What's that mean for us, lobo?"

"It means we must be ready. I don't think she's alone, and I think conflict burns in her heart. She was dear to me once, so I hope that isn't true. . ."

"We won't be caught unaware. But what's our next move out here?"

Merrill takes the man by the shoulders and turns him around, pointing beyond the desert in the direction of the Sierra Nevada mountains.

"There's a box canyon to the northwest. A remnant of the crown waits for us there."

Merrill's nostrils flare, and the wind brings to him a myriad of scents. His long hair whips in the harsh desert breeze, and he opens his mouth to let the taste of that long-forgotten crown piece settle onto his tongue.

"A gold miner traveled through there many years ago, and he carried that piece with him as a trinket, never knowing its significance. A rainstorm trapped him as he slept, and he drowned in that box canyon. The elements buried his remains, but the skeleton is still there, deep in the desert earth. And his sack of trinkets is buried next to his bones. It'll be an easy retrieval for this one. We dig, and we claim what belongs to us."

"When?"

"Eat and let the Coyotes rest. The journey through the Mojave has been long. The piece isn't going anywhere, and it'll keep for us. We'll go seeking in a few days."

Merrill brings the gristle of meat to his mouth, and he elongates his canines, irises turning to spiraling yellow as he chomps deep into the flesh of the thigh. Blood spurts from the corners of his mouth, and some of it drips down his fingers. He laps it off, lupine tongue sending pleasure spasms rolling along his spine. His eyes roll back to the whites in the sheer bliss of the moment.

Harvey Hollow watches in reverence.

"What's it like to taste meat as a wolf?"

"Multiply all the orgasms you've ever had in your life. Drape them in plasma and sinew. You taste the soul of what you're consuming. The life the creature had. The dreams reduced to tattered shreds of protein. . ."

Merrill favors his lieutenant with a grin so large that the corner of his mouth reaches back to his ear.

"You'll find out for yourself soon, Harvey Hollow."

They've been on the road for a few days, and they've made it as far as Newton, Kansas. They're stealth camping in a cornfield a few miles outside of the city, all three wolves nestled into their sleeping bags and staring up at the stars. They've been mostly on foot, and a few times they've managed to hitchhike in the backs of old farm trucks, but it's been slow going so far. Ivy can't help but worry that they're losing time.

Abel has his notepad out, and he's lazily scrawling sketches of the constellations above him. He's been doing well so far. She thought he'd become homesick, but it's mostly been a sense of almost childlike wonder for him. Seeing that there's a great big world beyond the homestead. Pyke is resting with his huge arms interlocked behind his head, a strip of cornhusk in his teeth.

"It's so damn flat out here. I miss the cover of trees. Is that weird?"

"No, Pyke. If anything, it's relatable. This is empty country."

Abel pipes up, a little smirk resting across his lips.

"Can't beat these stars though. The sky literally looks like a painting."

He rolls over onto his side and favors Ivy with a long contemplative glance.

"What's the update on Merrill?"

She lets her eyelids flutter closed, and she inhales deeply through her nose. The scent-bonded connection flows into her from thousands of miles away. She smells meat like roasted pork, but gamier. She smells restless sleepers and the ugliest nightmares playing in brainwashed heads. And beneath all of that, she smells him. She smells Merrill on his bedroll. She smells his long fingers caressing the unformed crown laid out across his sternum. She smells his obsession. And he senses she's locked in, so his lips pucker, and he blows a little kiss up into the air. She can almost taste that phantom kiss, his lips threatening to damn her.

She opens her eyes and shakes her head a little from side to side like a wet dog trying to dry itself.

"They haven't moved from their camp in the desert. But they're planning something. There's a reason they're staying there."

She swallows deeply, seeing comfort in the starlight.

"He knows we're coming. He and his ilk."

"Do you think he'll listen to reason?"

Ivy doesn't respond for a long time. She thinks of better days and a past full of tattered memories. She knew him once. She knew the wolf that Merrill *used* to be. . .

"I don't know."

They're making the pilgrimage to the box canyon on foot because there's no clear road through the badlands, and Merrill is keenly aware of how unforgiving this environment can be. Even with the enhanced endurance of a lycanthrope, he feels the thirst in the back of his throat and the sun beating down on the back of his neck. They frequently take breaks to guzzle down water, and while most would complain, his cannibals do not. He took around thirty of his Coyotes for the dig, and the rest are still at the camp. They're marching through the desert with pious obsession, and not a single one of them wants to be considered weak in the eyes of their wolfen messiah.

Harvey wears a balaclava around his face to help with the harsh grit of the desert wind, and he walks beside Merrill, making sure to crack the whip on stragglers that might be limping in the rear.

"Are we on the right track?"

"My nose never lies, Harvey Hollow. This scent is a siren song, and it screams for me."

Merrill looks skyward, and he sees vultures circling not far from their current position. The powerful aroma of carrion hits him, a side-scent compared to the focal point that is the crown piece, but it's enough to pique his interest.

"Slight detour, Harvey. The rest can forge on and we'll catch up. Come with me."

Harvey barks out a few orders to the Coyotes walking ahead, and then he splits off to follow Merrill along a little twisting game trail that breaks off into the scrub. They duck past cacti and trample through sagebrush, and soon they startle a cloud of flies, the buzzing bodies bursting up from their prize to avoid both Merrill and Harvey.

It's a bighorn sheep, the carcass bloated with putrescence. Merrill focuses on the eye sockets. The eyes are long gone, the gelatin picked clean, but maggots squiggle in those dark hollows, little newborn worms relishing their womb of decay.

Merrill feels the slobber in his mouth, and he makes no effort to control it. He lets it wash out past his lips to drip off his chin.

"I envy a maggot. Born in a wet, ruined place. Born from the dripping slop of death. There is nothing more pure, and I'll never turn down an invitation to join them for dinner."

As Merrill talks, he takes his clothes off, pants and shoes first, and then a slow unbuttoning of his shirt. He gently places these items into Harvey's hands after folding them, and he offers his acolyte a grin that is already growing.

From Harvey's perspective, the turn is like witnessing a dark miracle. He watches as Merrill's arms contort, the musculature rippling outward, sleek black fur sprouting from pores, his legs lengthening as his height is enhanced, his hands twitching as fingers become massive paws with bone-colored claws. The head transformation is last, the human features melting like clay as the shaggy canine head of the wolf burns up to the surface, and Merrill's face is suddenly all snout, bottomless black eyes, and row after row of razor teeth.

The wolf speaks, and his voice is warped music.

"A little protein snack for the road ahead, Harvey Hollow."

He turns from his acolyte, upper lip twitching into a snarl, and then he falls on the carcass of the bighorn sheep, burying his mouth into the maggot-infested meat and slurping and biting and burrowing until his whole head is in a stinking wound on the sheep's abdomen.

Harvey watches the feast, and Merrill pulls a handful of rotten flesh from the carcass and tosses it back to him. Hollow barely manages to catch the foulness, tiny white worms squiggling across it.

He smashes it into his mouth with greedy enthusiasm, chewing and smiling all the while. It is vile, but Harvey relishes the vile. This is what animals do.

And being an animal has always been Harvey's greatest aspiration in life.

CHAPTER 9

Utah is all natural splendor, rock outcroppings that reach valiantly into the clouds, and expanses of horizon that seem to stretch on forever. Abel is like a babe fresh from the womb, gawking at everything, and Pyke can't help but chuckle at him as he furiously scrawls notes and sketches into his Moleskine pad. They're on the road again, their boots treading backroads, and the sun feels warm and welcome on Ivy's freckled shoulders.

But Ivy knows in her heart that the good weather and equally good vibes can't last. Nevada is getting closer and closer, and, with it, the fiends who have gathered deep in the Mojave. She's scented Merrill's movements a few times in the last few days of travel, and she knows that he's gone deeper into the badlands, but they're covering no great distance, so he and his cannibals must be on foot.

They have to be searching for something out there, and if it's another piece of the crown, then time is of the essence. She can't risk him finding another shard of that relic. She can't risk him spilling more blood without even the most rudimentary feeling of remorse.

She wonders what he's like now. It's been years since she's seen Merrill, and time changes people. She doesn't doubt that time changes wolves too, and it's clear that Merrill's fangs haven't dulled. If anything, the circumstances of his life have sharpened those canines, made him close off some part of himself that used to be capable of compassion. It hurts her to think of that. As awful as he's become, his deeds now infamous among the superpack, she wants to believe that he's just lost in some inexpressible way. Hurting because of being cut off from his home, when his kin so grievously hurt him first. . .

She has to be strong when the time comes. She can't assume that he's the wolf she once considered thoughtful, intelligent, and driven to a level of ambition that went beyond even the borders of Merkel Valley. Those positive attributes have been inverted. At some point in the time that has elapsed since he left the homestead, his moral compass was dropped to the dirt and crushed beneath his heel.

But the greatest question of all eats at her as she hikes alongside her brethren, giving them brief smiles and snippets of small talk when she's really inside of her own head.

Is that moral compass repairable?

Seeing the box canyon is like entering the terrain of an alien world, and Merrill finds himself in awe of the layout of the place. Steep vertical walls carved by the passage of time, and the entrance tight and intimate, a mouth opening into a darkened throat. He is not pureborn, so there was a time when he was still human before the turn, and he remembers once when he tried heroin as a troubled youth. Only an isolated incident at a party, the strange euphoria of that drug burning through his bloodstream. He knew it was bad news and never tried it again, but what is in his nostrils now is comparable.

The shard of crown stinks of euphoria. It is forgotten, eldritch bliss carried through the cool breeze within the confines of the canyon walls. His brain quivers with pleasure at the thought of finding it, and even though the crown is an inanimate object, it's clear that it *wants* to be whole again.

He sent a number of his cannibals in to scout, and so far they've cleared out debris that might impede progress, including deadfalls and small animal dens. They've been sandbagging a portion of swampy quicksand that would prove problematic if not dealt with. Merrill and Harvey have been lingering near the entrance, but Merrill can feel his patience starting to run out. He needs to be in there. He needs to sniff out what rightfully belongs to him. . .

But he has more to worry about than just finding the crown piece. That other familiar scent is drawing closer, cutting through the miles that separate them with each hour that passes. He smells her freckles, the follicles of her hair, and the misguided sycophants that travel with her. Ivy's scent overwhelms and distracts him, and her timing couldn't be more irritating.

He approaches Harvey, seeing his chief Coyote standing there in the shadows of a Joshua tree and looking down at the contents of a large pack that was brought along on the trek. The objects gleam in the sunlight, reflective hunks of metal. It's an old medieval suit of armor broken down into pieces, each section battered and sporting dents. Helmet, breastplate, gauntlets, etc.

"What do you have in mind for that antique, Harvey?"

The man looks up, his gaze momentarily far away like he was just stirred from a dream. Merrill simply stares at himself in the mirrored aviators, his head cocking slightly to the side.

"With your permission, I'd like The Chemist to work on it. He has silver nitrate in his possession. It's solid, like a sand. It could be smelted and worked into the armor. It might give us an edge if those unfriendly wolves try to spoil the party."

The Chemist is probably one of the more peculiar cannibals in the clan. Merrill has always thought the man looks a bit like a human shrew. He was in the meth trade before he joined them, and his face was badly injured in a lab explosion at some point. His features are all melted pink gloop and shifty hazel eyes.

"If I allow this, I'll be putting a great deal of trust in you. You'll have to keep the silver away from me. It wounds a wolf terribly."

"And with enough enthusiasm, it is fatal, my lobo. But the armor will never even come close to you. I'll use what hurts you the most. . .to protect you against those that do not share our vision."

"So be it. Let The Chemist work his magic. Who will don the armor if it becomes necessary to make a stand? Do you have someone in mind?"

Harvey Hollow immediately drops to a knee before Merrill, kneeling in reverence to his leader.

"I'd like the honor."

Merrill can't help but smile. He lifts a hand, allowing his fingers to elongate, the claws becoming more pronounced. He uses this hand to tap the claws against both of Harvey's shoulders.

"Consider yourself knighted."

CHAPTER 10

"I don't like this, Ivy. It feels claustrophobic."

Abel stares up at the ragged walls of the box canyon, the trio working their way through the twists and turns that lead deeper into it. They made record time getting through the Mojave, and Ivy thinks that is largely due to the fact that the closer she got to Merrill, the more she felt compelled to see him and have this long overdue confrontation.

But there's caution in their blood. Even Pyke—usually a stoic soul who puts on a brave face—seems shaken while trying to navigate his big body through the tight channel of the canyon.

All three wolves hear the grunts of Merrill's disciples up ahead. They hear shovels descending and piercing the earth. It's clear that his cannibals have been working feverishly, but have they unearthed what they're hunting for? She can't be sure, but she hopes that there's still time.

They round a bend, and all three of them stop dead in their tracks. The sounds have stopped completely. No more groans of exertion, and no more sounds of picks and shovels battling against the hardpan. About fifty feet ahead of them, the box canyon is choked off with bodies. The Coyotes stand like leering human shields, and Ivy has no doubt that Merrill positioned them to be exactly that. They're a sour, ragged lot, clothed in threadbare garments, their skin sallow and sun-chapped, and she sees that a few of them have even filed their teeth to points, no doubt trying to impress their wolfen master.

She estimates that about twenty of them are present, and from behind them, barely visible from the wall of cannibals he has guarding him, is Merrill Sade. She hasn't seen him in years. His hair is longer, his face more weathered, and if it's even possible, it seems like his eyes have darkened to represent what has been festering in his soul.

It bothers her deeply that if she had seen him elsewhere in a public place, she might not have recognized him at all. He's much changed, and is that true of his heart as well?

"Even from hundreds of miles away, I knew it was your scent, Ivy. It's fitting that they sent you. . ."

She raises her voice to bridge the distance, and Pyke and Abel both maintain defensive stances.

"Merrill, please. I just want to palaver. Can we talk privately?"

The rogue wolf lifts his arms and opens them wide, and she can just see him back there grinning behind his cannibals.

"There's no need for that. These are my kindred. Eaters of flesh and eaters of knowledge. Aren't they beautiful? They yearn to live as lupines."

Pyke steps forward now, his jaw tightening.

"You blaspheme, Merrill. You spit in the face of Mother Moon with these deviants. Call them off, and let's just sit down somewhere and talk like wolves."

"Pyke, ol' boy. You're far from home. Negotiation isn't one of your strengths. Maybe you should have stayed behind to mend farming tools, since that is about all that you're good for."

A low snarl starts in the back of Pyke's throat, and Ivy quickly steps forward to grab his shoulder and pull the big man backward.

"You have innocent blood beneath your claws. For the sake of what we once had, let me help you, Merrill. We'll figure this out. . ."

Merrill laughs, a throaty chuckle that echoes through the box canyon. A few of the Coyotes laugh with him, mad titters from equally mad souls.

"Help me? But you've come to *hinder* me! Your rigid little rules, that commune up in the hills full of drum circles and wolves that eat more greens than meat. I'm not speaking to *carnivores*. You've let Braun and that damn place neuter and spay all three of you. Simpering pacifists coming to me with hats in hands. You have forgotten yourselves. You deny instinct. You deny the very nature of what it means to be a lycanthrope. . ."

There's so much disgust in Merrill's voice, a dripping and ceaseless disappointment.

"Enough. We are three wolves, and you are but one, Merrill. You know these mortals won't stand long against all three of us if bloodshed is what you're after."

Merrill lifts a hand to his chin, rubbing it thoughtfully. The Coyotes slobber and grin in front of him, the cannibals almost twitching at the thought of proving their mettle.

"You underestimate the power of numbers, Ivy. But don't worry—"

The rogue wolf throws back his head, and he unleashes with an ear-splitting howl that makes pebbles fall down from the walls of the box canyon. The cannibals start to become even more agitated, barking and screaming right along with their master.

"—I'll teach you."

The next few moments come in a chaotic flash. Merrill tilts his chin in the direction of the trio, and the cannibals pour forth as one united horde. Pyke moves quickly, putting his own body in front of Ivy and Abel, and he's already in the process of turning as he does this. Shaggy gray fur bursts from his pores, his fingers turn to knives, and the canines become like railroad spikes in his mouth. His head contorts until he's in lupine form, a barrel-chested wolf with ears laid back across his skull.

The first few bodies to hit Pyke become mincemeat. His teeth and claws are like a whirlwind, tearing and splashing the walls of the box canyon in gore. Entrails fly, organs are unhoused, and human carcasses open themselves to him until his fur is soaked in red. But the Coyotes are many, and soon they're jumping atop him en masse, rusted little knives finding his hide, dirty fingers tearing at his ears and his eyes. A dogpile of stinking bodies overwhelm the great wolf, but still he fights, and their best efforts are merely superficial. Ivy and Abel try to jump in, but they're fending off cannibals of their own, so entrenched in a close-quarters melee that they haven't even found the time to fully transform.

Pyke turns to them, a cannibal wrapped around his huge wolfen head and biting into his ear with scummy black teeth, and he flicks the man free before roaring to his kin.

"Climb the wall and make for the top of the canyon! I'll hold them. I'll meet you there!"

No sooner has Pyke said that than the horde starts to cleave itself in two, allowing a new contender to walk through the huge group of ragged vagabonds. Merrill stays far back from the action, but he ushers his lieutenant onward.

Harvey Hollow is death itself suited in silver. He wears gauntlets, a breastplate, and a helmet of medieval armor, all of it infused in silver nitrate. He gleams in the sunlight that filters down from above, and in his hands is a halberd that has been wrapped up tight in strands of silver-infused barbwire.

Pyke sees Harvey coming, and his struggles against the cannibals that are piling atop him become even more ferocious. He throws a paw in the direction of the box-canyon wall, urging Ivy and Abel to climb before time runs out.

"Go!"

Ivy is trying to push past a fat cannibal with a face eaten up by gangrene, his broken teeth snapping at her, but Abel yanks her backward and tosses her up onto a lip of the rock. His claws elongate half-formed, and he starts to scrabble up the face of the canyon.

"Don't let his sacrifice be in vain, Ivy! There are too many," Abel barked.

Pyke succeeds in throwing off the last of the cannibals bedeviling him, and he makes a beeline straight for Harvey. Instead of flinching, Hollow ducks a massive claw swipe from Pyke and sends a balled, gauntleted fist smashing up into the underside of his jaw. The silver burns like fire, and Pyke staggers back against a box-canyon wall, scratching at his own hairy chin and shaking his head from side to side in pain. Several more cannibals burst forward onto Pyke, ripping out handfuls of fur and throwing ineffectual punches into his torso. He takes hold of one and bites the woman's head, crunching her skull and allowing her boneless body to accordion down in front of him, but Hollow uses the distraction to run up and send several stiff knee shots into Pyke's abdomen, the silver plating of his knee-guards causing steam to drift up after each blow that connects.

Pyke rakes at Hollow, leaving huge claw marks on his breastplate, and the armored man is knocked back a few steps, struggling to use his halberd for balance. The wounded werewolf bellows, his mouth opening wide as he goes for the killing bite on Harvey's throat, but the man's reflexes are keen, and he catches Pyke by the tongue, silver-gauntlet fingers causing such a caustic sting on the sensitive flesh that Pyke pushes himself away to gain relief. He begins to violently cough and clutch at his mouth, and Harvey sees his opening, and he decides to take it.

Hollow steps confidently forward and thrusts the halberd up into Pyke's chest just beneath the ribcage. There's a hideous sizzling sound, and a deep glaze enters Pyke's eyes. The big werewolf lashes out with his right paw, the blow knocking Hollow's helmet clean off his head, but the cannibal recovers. He wears a chainmail headpiece underneath, and even his aviator shades. One lens is cracked, and with teeth gritted, Harvey pushes the halberd up higher into Pyke's sternum. The silver reaches his heart, and the anguish of it forces a howl out of Pyke's purpled lips. He tries once more to swipe a claw at Hollow's head, but he's so weak that the cannibal catches his wrist and slams it back against the canyon wall.

He leans close, and Pyke can see his own dying visage in the reflection of Harvey Hollow's aviators. Blood is pouring down from his snout and mouth, and each breath he takes is like an inhalation of razorblades.

Abel is almost dragging Ivy up the side of the canyon wall, cannibals below jumping up and trying to grasp their ankles, and she reaches for Pyke, her face torn with emotion.

Hollow takes hold of Pyke's chin with his gauntlet, lifting the wolf's head so that they're eye to eye. He takes in a deep whiff of burnt hair and charring meat, the silver acting like an acid when exposed to the lupine flesh.

"It's not personal. You're a majestic creature. I hate to put you down. It's just that on this occasion, you chose the wrong side."

Hollow stabs the halberd even deeper and *twists* it, embedding the blade into the rock face on the other side of Pyke's body. The wolf expires before it's even done. His lupine form fades into itself, almost like the reverse bloom of a flower, and what is left is his human form, a large blacksmith painted in bruises and blood.

Abel and Ivy make it to the top of the box canyon, and they both flop forward, gasping from exertion. More cannibals are running across the desert hardpan in their direction, and Abel manages to half-transform and slice a throat clean before he's clocked on the back of the head with a huge rock. He falls to all fours, badly stunned, and Ivy is about to join the fight before two sly lycanthrope arms slip around her neck from behind and begin to choke her out, flailing her body from side to side in a sleeper hold. She falls to the earth, dust clouds billowing, and in the dust she sees the leering werewolf face of Merrill staring down at her. He slobbers and he grins, cannibal reinforcements gathering behind him. A little urchin with a boil on his neck turns to the lycan leader, sounding almost excited when he asks his question.

"Do we bleed them, master?"

Merrill leans down, one yellowed claw brushing a few locks of Ivy's hair behind her ear.

"Spare them. They are lambs. Nothing of the wolf is left inside. I see that now."

Ivy wishes she could summon enough strength to spit in his face, but before she can, she passes out.

CHAPTER 11

Half-formed images come to Ivy, all of them blurry and broken, barely tangible. Cannibals working at Pyke's body with knives and hatchets, chopping, dismembering, and most importantly, decapitating. Manacles with little outer-rim silver teeth being slipped around her wrists so that when she rustles them too much, the silver bites into the skin and starts in motion a caustic burn.

The feeling of her body being dragged, heels scraping against the desert hardpan. Merrill returned to his human form, crouching near where the box canyon ends with a massive pit there in front of him. Harvey Hollow and a cannibal called The Chemist standing next to him. She remembers floating up from unconsciousness long enough to feel her stomach turn at the state of The Chemist's face. Features all twisted scar tissue from chemical burns, skin like pink melted candle wax.

Merrill's fingers sifting through dirt, mummified clothing, and bones that crumble when he touches them. And then a tremor in his body, his eyes rolling to the whites, and his hand closing around a piece of broken stone. He plucks the artifact up and marvels at it, his infernal crown that much closer to being completed.

Fractured dialogue coming to her from all sides, echoes of the damned.

"A king's crown. Pulled from death and dust."

"How does it feel, my lobo?"

"Closer. Closer still."

"We're almost there."

"It stinks of a buried god. He who once used elder hemlocks to pick his teeth with. He growls again, and he growls through me. A wolf skull the size of a continent beneath a dead cherry tree."

Ivy tries to rouse herself, feeling like she's locked in some half-awake nightmare world full of delusions, but her thoughts are too thick, and it feels like her blood has turned to molasses. She's dimly aware of Abel's warm body somewhere near her, and before she's able to try anything else, consciousness abandons her again.

She awakens sometime later to her prone body rattling on a thin mattress. Her thoughts are muddy, her reflexes slow, and even the wolf within seems catatonic. She can see that she's in the interior of an RV that's moving along a road, but that's about the extent of it. Merrill sits on a stool next to her, and he's in the process of warming a rag in a bucket of water. He reaches out and wets her forehead with it, wiping away some of the desert grime and the droplets of perspiration.

"Tranquilizer used for big game animals. Mostly grizzlies. I hate to do it, Ivy, but after that stunt in the canyon, I have to take precautions. You're gonna feel groggy, and I want the beast in you to sleep."

She mumbles, reaching up with the intention to grab his collar and pull his head down so she can get her teeth into him. It's no good. Her fingers barely brush clumsily against his chest before her arm flops back to her side.

"Where you taking us? Where's Abel?"

Her voice doesn't even sound like it belongs to her, her words incoherent and slurred.

"Abel will keep. He's resting, and he needs it after all of that unnecessary trauma. Why couldn't you just let me go? You had to interfere."

"I came to reason with you. To pull you off the ledge, and to remind myself that you can't be what they say you are. You can't be that fucking heartless. And in seconds of us reuniting, you confirm to me that you *are*. You had your filth kill Pyke, you murdering—"

She wants to continue, but Merrill presses his hand gently against her slurring lips, closing them up so that her speech is muffled.

"We defended ourselves. Pyke had bloodshed infecting his brain, and I could smell it the moment he stepped in front of me. He was cocksure and itching for violence."

He takes his hand away, and she can feel her eyelids fluttering closed again. It feels like there are heavy weights on her chest, and if she gives in to them, all will be well again. Maybe the events in the canyon were just a dream, and she'll wake up in Merkel Valley.

"You're lost, Merrill."

Swimming again, churning the waters of sleep or the lands that border sleep.

"So lost."

She dreams in memory.

Ivy is back at the homestead, and she's a teen, all gangly limbs and burgeoning hormones. She'd been holding Merrill in her arms, supporting his slim frame as she used tweezers to pluck buckshot out of his thigh and arm. She dropped the little pieces of shrapnel into a mason jar filled with lukewarm water, and she brushed the sweaty mop of hair out of his eyes.

They'd been dating for around a year, but Ivy had her eye on him even when they were younger. Merrill came to them as a child instead of being born in Merkel Valley like her. He was an orphan, and he'd been stealth camping in a state park and foraging in dumpsters for food. A wolf passed through, and it tore through the little boy's camp as he slept. All he remembers is that the wolf was an albino, and it was gargantuan. But it didn't eat him, seemed to have no intention of that. Instead, that massive albino took his little boy face into its mouth and gave it the gentlest bite, just barely breaking the skin. Merrill said that he remembers the wolf leaning down, licking his ear, and whisper-growling to him. It had glimmering Nordic eyes and braids in its shaggy fur.

"I'm called Endre. When you're older and your fangs grow, find me, boy. I'll show you the way."

And with that, the wolf was gone, and the little boy was left to bleed and cry in the dead leaves. Merrill said that he searched far and wide after that, but he never found the great white wolf again. It was like he never existed at all. But he did find others of his kind. He found Merkel Valley, and he learned what it meant to be a wolf.

Ivy liked the boy from the start. He was so inquisitive, eager to learn all that he could. He seemed to want to consume knowledge and savor it just as much as his meat.

And that curiosity often got him into trouble. It led him to the outer rim of their territory, and it led Merrill beyond the homestead. He told her he'd just been running in the woods and he lost track of time, enjoying the wind tousling through his fur, relishing the freedom of being connected to nature.

He took to being a wolf like no other. It was his true calling. It was like he was never even meant to be human, that was just the cocoon he had to survive in order to become the butterfly that he was always destined to be. So when he came upon the turkey hunters out there in their orange hats and flannel jackets, he didn't think twice about how he was in lupine form. He stood up on his hind legs, and he put out a steadying hand to them. He spoke, his voice a pleasant canine purr.

"No reason to fear me, brothers. I'll do no harm."

Ivy kept plucking the buckshot out of him, and she remembers the emotion in Merrill's eyes as he told her this. His youthful features strained to contain some level of composure, but his heart was beating fast, and she could feel how flushed his skin was. How enraged and betrayed he felt.

"They never even blinked, Ivy. They just raised their guns up, and they shot. I didn't retaliate. I just ran. These bullets are nothing to me. These bullets are like bee stings. That isn't what hurt. What hurt is how they looked at me. . ."

Ivy watched him swallow, his Adam's apple bobbing.

"They looked at me with hate. Blind, idiotic hate. They didn't want to understand. They didn't want to learn. It was like my very existence offended them. Like the fact that I walked and communicated challenged everything that allowed them to live in their polished societies. But why, Ivy? They're animals too. They've just forgotten. . ."

She remembers his snarl, and she remembers looking away so that she wouldn't make him feel worse by seeing the tears shining in his eyes.

"But I'll never forget. I'll never forget their hate."

Ivy awakens choking on the stench of sour earth, and it takes everything in her willpower not to flop forward and vomit into her own lap. Her eyelids are crusted over from sleep, and she has to squint to make out the interior of where she is. She's chained down to a large rusty eyebolt in the center of a dome-shaped room, and the silver manacles are still on her wrists, preventing her from wiggling around too much without pressing those burning teeth into her flesh. Abel breathes next to her, kneeling on his knees in grime, and she can just make out a smear of dried maroon across his split eyebrow. His lupine nature has already caused the wound to stitch itself and heal, but the remnants remain there caked onto his skin. Her night vision finally kicks in, and she's able to see more of the gloom surrounding them.

The floor itself is vile. It's sloppy, oozing mud, earth so black that it's almost sickly sweet, and there is trash everywhere. Broken bottles, discarded bags, and even items of a more unsavory nature. Spent condoms tossed into corners, empty syringes cracked under boot heels, and the sense that this is a hopeless place designed to attract hopeless souls. The walls are crumbling concrete, and they're marred in graffiti. Crude artwork like human genitalia, gang tags, cryptic messages that seem to have no clear meaning.

Abel watches her in the dark, head hanging and forlorn. She hears Merrill's cannibals all around her in other rooms and sunken chambers, the filth seeming right at home in a place like this.

"Fort Armistead. It's a decommissioned military base that was abandoned in 1920. They took the gun batteries away, and they left it to rot in the forest. All that's left now is a concrete foundation and these stinking catacombs. These chambers never see the sun, Ivy. Merrill likes that just fine."

She tries to rouse herself, feeling like her head was just smacked around a few hundred times with a grizzly bear paw.

"You know this place? Whereabouts is it?"

"I was drugged for most of the trip, but I've read about this place, so I know it well. We're just outside of Baltimore, Maryland. A seedy little stretch of land that the city left to just slowly degrade into itself. He's made camp down here. How can a wolf stand this? It's a decaying eyesore, and it offends the nose. It smells of sour thoughts and mental decline."

"That's all Merrill is now, Abel. Sour thoughts and mental decline. I was a fool to think we'd be able to just have a conversation and work things out. If I had known for just an instant how bad things have gotten, there's a chance Pyke would still be—"

The sob starts low in the back of her throat, and it cuts off her words. Abel reaches out and his fingertips are just barely able to graze her bare shoulder, providing what little comfort to her that he can.

"You had the best intentions. Pyke knew what he was signing up for, and it wasn't your fault. If anything, we've learned what we're up against. Merrill pissed on even the idea of an olive branch being extended to him."

"How long have you been awake? Has anyone been in here?"

"The one they call The Chemist brings us food and water each day. You've been in and out for almost forty-eight hours. I have no idea why we're here or what they plan to do."

Abel reaches behind himself for a wooden bowl filled with lukewarm meat and potatoes, along with a jug of water about half full. He offers both to Ivy, and she's so ravenous that she immediately begins to dig in, washing down each bite with gulps of water. Her throat feels parched, dryer than the desert from whence they came.

"This is bad, Ivy. We need to somehow get word to Braun. Even if we managed to escape, there are just too damn many of them for us to be able to even make a dent."

Ivy stops eating with a hunk of beef pinched between her fingers. She cuts her eyes to Abel, and she hears hollow footsteps approaching down the opposite end of the chamber.

The imprisoned wolves have a visitor.

His boots squelch in the fetid muck, and when The Chemist appears before them, both wolves instinctually bare their teeth. He kneels down, holding some contraption in his hands, and he stares at them. His face is like a ruined portrait, all sloppy melted scars, and he stinks of the same vileness that is beneath their feet. Wet earth and spoiled nightcrawlers. Ivy struggles not to vomit in the presence of this man.

"Abel, I'm told you're a learned man. You appreciate history? I've made you a present. It's called a Heretic's Fork."

The Chemist lifts up the object for both of them to get a good look at. It's a leather collar with two meat forks attached on opposite ends, but one of the forks gleams with silver, and just being in close proximity to the element gives both Ivy and Abel extreme anxiety.

"The Spanish Inquisition enjoyed using these. One fork rests against the sternum, and the other presses close to the underside of the chin. They're not lethal, but they inflict great pain. I've made a few adjustments to this one so that you'll still be able to converse. The silver fork will rest under your chin. . ."

The Chemist leans forward and wraps the collar around Abel's throat, taking time to buckle it. Abel tries to violently yank his neck back, but The Chemist wags his finger from side to side in a tsk-tsk gesture.

"Mister Sade wants to speak, and this will ensure that you behave like a good doggie during that conversation. Don't let your head hang too low lest the silver pierce your chin. It's important that you give him your full attention."

Ivy thrusts her head forward, trying to put her own body in front of Abel's to block him out of view for the moment.

"Why do you people follow him? What compels you?"

The Chemist looks at her like he's profoundly confused. One of his arms is a twisted branch of bone that must be held close to his chest, the flesh charred to the point of being like old leather.

"Because being a wolf is the closest thing to tasting divinity. We must earn the turn. We must prove our worth so that one day we can become like Mister Sade. I relish the thought of casting aside this frail mortal cage in favor of the animal inside."

The Chemist looks almost dreamy. One of his eyes is a dim cataract, but the healthy one twinkles with emotion.

"And when I ascend, when the beast I've always been is free, my wounds will heal. It is rebirth."

"Merrill's tongue is forked, and he is a very eloquent liar. I don't blame you. There was a time when I once swallowed his lies too. I swallowed them because they were sweet to the taste. But you'll learn that it doesn't last with him."

The Chemist stares at her like he's offended.

"Mister Sade will soon be a god. It is a stupid thing to speak ill of a god."

Abel tries to quiet Ivy, shaking his head silently while staring at the grimy earth he crouches on.

"Don't bother, Ivy. These people are cult members. He's got them brainwashed."

The Chemist reaches down and pulls Abel to his feet by the manacles on his wrist, the skinny wolf trying hard to keep his head held back so that the metal ends of the silver fork won't stab up into the bottom of his chin. Ivy darts forth, growling protectively, and The Chemist quickly steps back as soon as her eyes take on a yellow lamplight glow.

"You're a hardy she-wolf, and I don't underestimate your bite. But it would be unwise for you to transform while wearing those manacles. I designed them myself. If you turn, those silver spikes will shred through your wrists in minutes. I know wolves can heal in miraculous ways, but even a wolf can't regrow a pair of paws once they've been burnt down to nubs. Trust me, Ivy. I know a thing or two about burning."

He brushes his fingertips across the melted candle-wax skin of his face, and he smiles at her. It's a putrid smile, a rat grinning in the gloom.

He begins to shove Abel in the direction of another catacomb entrance, and she's just able to reach out and squeeze her friend's hand before he's gone from her sight.

Ivy hopes like hell that she hasn't seen the last of him.

The first thing Abel notices is the sound of chewing. The catacombs are mazelike, stagnant water dripping down from cracks in the ceiling, huge broken fissures in the concrete walls, and so much garbage strewn around that you'd think they were walking in an underground landfill.

He is ushered into a small chamber, and there's an old antique barber's chair in the middle of the room. It leans to the side, sagging and derelict, but when The Chemist shoves him down into it, Abel is thankful to at least be sitting instead of standing. It takes some pressure off the Heretic's Fork that longs to jam itself into his skin.

It's very dark, and it takes a moment for Abel to see with his wolf eyes. The night vision shows him things he'd be better off not seeing. Merrill stands before him, hands rubbing together, a warm smirk resting on his lips. Harvey Hollow leans against a column close to his master, the lieutenant absently running his hands along the mutilation scars that decorate his arms. And behind both men, the wet smacking sounds of eating. It's hard for Abel to see from his vantage point, but it appears that the cannibals are crouched down and eating one of their own people. It's all gleaming red viscera and filthy hands plunging down into puncture holes. They slurp up guts like noodles, and they carve little slivers off the torso of the body with butter knives, pausing to slide these morsels across their tongues.

Merrill looks back at the scene, pausing to chuckle a bit. He seems to appreciate the fact that the Coyotes are eating their meal raw.

"I'm sorry about that, Abel. It was a long trip out of the desert, and they get very hungry."

"They're eating one of their own. You condone this?"

"He was sick and wounded from the battle with Pyke. I don't just condone it, I encourage it. Why not cannibalize the weak amongst you? It's nature, Abel. The strong eat and flourish, the weak do not. It maintains the balance."

Merrill shrugs his shoulders, strolling a bit in front of Abel's chair to stretch his legs.

"If it's my time, I'd rather go out with the teeth and tongues of my kindred embracing me. That brings comfort. It warms my heart to know that I'll live and die as an animal. You don't share that same vision?"

Abel looks disgusted, his back arched as he struggles to find a position in the barber's chair that will give him some kind of relief from the collar around his neck. He's unable to find such a position.

"It's barbaric. There's nothing civil in that. We're capable of thinking and feeling like men. The wolf inside is a gift to be thankful for, but we learn self-control in Merkel Valley. You were never very good at self-control."

"Preaching to the choir! You forget I was there. I learned plenty. And what ugly, restrictive lessons there are to learn in that little commune. I always thought you were different, Abel. When I was young, I saw you as a teacher. A mentor. Someone that wanted more out of life than Braun's moon-worshipping bullshit routine where we all pick flowers together and farm and eat tasteless deer meat every single night to prove how wild and free we are. That's not the behavior of a wolf. That's the behavior of a leashed dog that has lived so long in a house that he doesn't even understand what the outside is anymore."

Abel feels the muscles in his neck weakening, but he struggles to hold his head up, beads of sweat starting to collect across his brow.

"I remember a boy who fell in love with literature. A quiet boy that found solace in books when the world became too harsh to bear. Is he still in there, Merrill? Does that boy still breathe?"

Merrill leans closer and places both of his hands on the armrests of the barber's chair, dark locks of hair hanging about his face. His eyes drift up to the cracks in the ceiling, his expression almost unreadable.

"I remember him too. I was with that boy when he was banished from the only home he'd ever known. I was with him when he was told that knowledge is a sin and his thoughts and dreams should be confined to a small box. I shivered with him alone in meadows coated in frost. I cried with him in the musty corners of abandoned factories as he tried to sleep the sad away. I walked with that young wolf after he lost everything. His friends, his support, his pack, gone like smoke in a breeze."

Merrill's gaze grows hard and jaded. His trip down memory lane seems to be causing him considerable emotional pain, and Abel is surprised because he didn't even think the man capable of feeling anything anymore.

"That boy had his time wandering the wilderness. I'll never forget that boy, Abel. And I hope that you never forget that when I was cast out and you all turned your backs on me, I was still *only* a boy. Lost, confused, and yearning for meaning. I never found it in Merkel Valley. I never found that acceptance with you or any of the meek and toothless wolves that den there. But as I prowled this world alone, I found something better."

Merrill grits his teeth, his mouth mere inches from Abel's nose. He seems almost tempted to bite right into his face and shred the scholar's features into messy red strands.

"I found Apollo Lykaios, and I have never looked back."

Abel's face constricts, and he feels that he's losing the battle to hold his head high and maintain eye contact with Merrill.

"If I was your teacher, I failed you, Merrill. I see that now. I'm so sorry for what you've become."

His strength fades, and Abel's head drops, the silver fork piercing up into the underside of his chin. There's a foul sizzling followed by steam billowing from the wound, and Abel howls in agony, thrashing his head from side to side before lifting it up and away from the fork.

Merrill casually takes a step forward and plunges a hand down against Abel's scalp, wrapping up a fistful of his hair to help him hold his head up so that it won't connect with the Heretic's Fork again.

"Forgiveness is something that must be earned. You know this place, don't you? It's familiar to you."

Abel breathes deeply, trying to gulp down some of the pain, a few tendrils of steam still drifting up from the wound beneath his chin.

"I read about it. It's just an old fort. There's nothing special here."

Merrill lifts up his head and sniffs the air, nostrils flaring deeply. He does this for a few moments, taking his time with it, scenting all that there is to be scented.

"On the surface, I'm inclined to agree with you. I smell desperate sexual acts performed at three in the morning, and tears after. I smell drugs. Heroin, meth, coke, all those naughty adult treats. I smell black mud and all the blackened souls that have walked on it. Body odor, raccoon shit, and dead doves with broken and half-eaten wings. My nose tells me all of those things. But there is a smell beyond those things. A deep, dark *undersmell.* That smell has never lied to me, Abel. It's the smell of a crown piece."

Merrill's grip on Abel's hair tightens a little more, and he moves his head down just a bit closer to the silver fork that gleams around his neck.

"And I think you know more than you're saying. I can't identify *where* that smell is coming from, and it drives me crazy. I've prowled every inch of these catacombs and I've found nothing. But perhaps a bright bookish fellow like you can enlighten me. And if not? Well, silver is a great motivator."

Merrill steps back and allows Abel's head to drop, and the fork stabs up into the fresh wound that has formed there, burning and sending caustic waves of pain through Abel's system. He screams and he screams and he screams, and his screams echo all the way down to Ivy's chamber.

She shivers in her sleep and does her best to clamp her hands up over her ears to dampen the sound.

CHAPTER 14

Abel staggers down the steps, the wounds from the Heretic's Fork sending shockwaves of pain into his stressed anatomy. Merrill, Harvey, and The Chemist all follow behind him, the two cannibals occasionally stepping forward to help shove Abel along if he slows down while Merrill hangs back and watches. His boots squish through grime that is like quicksand at the bottom of the stairs, and pulling his feet free each step requires effort. He stumbles forward, manacled hands held out in front of him. The collar with the Heretic's Fork has been mercifully removed, and The Chemist has tucked it into his knapsack for now.

Abel stops at a dead-end, nothing but a wall there with stonework that is mossy and glistening with water. He steps to the side to allow the others to get a good look, and then he hangs his head and motions to a particular stone that juts out a little awkwardly. He found out about this in one of the forbidden texts at Merkel Valley, and he had hoped that he'd be able to keep the secret from Merrill, but torture involving silver stabbing up into his flesh over and over again loosened his tongue, and now he has no choice.

"Press the stone and twist your wrist just slightly to the left."

Merrill grunts, and Harvey pushes forward and does just that, palming the slick stone before giving it a twist. There's a rattling sound, and suddenly the wall slides open, presenting a dark gap leading into a little rounded room. Dust and lichen rains down, and all of them cough a bit and cover their mouths with their sleeves before peering inside.

"You first."

Harvey grabs Abel by the back of his neck and pushes him through. The prisoner trips and falls down to his hands and knees near a short altar in the center of the room. It's inlaid with old claw marks, and on top is a rotting satin pillow. A shard of the crown sits in a bed of dust and cobwebs atop the pillow, and Merrill makes a beeline for it, his nostrils flaring as a wolfish grin overtakes his face.

"You sneaky devil. What a dirty and delicious little secret you've been keeping from us," said Merrill.

Everyone crowds into the chamber, and they take in more of the interior. The ceiling is all carved and polished stonework, and it depicts a mural. There are black obsidian claws, huge hooked fangs, and feral eyes that glow rabid in the gloom. It showcases the entire world as one big hunting ground with roaming packs of wolves consuming anything and everything. As Abel stares up at the mural, he can't help but feel his bowels tighten inside of him. What is depicted up there is unsustainable chaos. It's life being eaten and chewed and glutted upon. A perverse homage to Apollo Lykaios.

Merrill has his neck craned back, admiring the intricate details of the mural, and it's clear that he's swooning. His hand reaches out absently, and he rescues the crown piece from its forgotten nest, the material of the pillow crumpling inward as he does so. As soon as his fingers make contact, his mind is flooded with sensations and images. Human sacrifice. Brutal blood orgies in old-growth forests. Wolves and humans frolicking together around enormous bonfires. Endless meat, endless teeth, and appetites that yearn everlasting. It's an assault on his senses, and he welcomes it with open arms.

When he finally comes back to himself, he notices that slobber is pooling from his mouth. Merrill swipes at it, eyes finally rolling down from the whites, and he casts his attention back to his cannibals. Abel withers in horror, and having read the forbidden texts himself, he knows all too well about the eldritch power that Merrill is experiencing.

"He calls to me. He growls across dimensional voids. I can feel his claws scraping against the fabric of our reality. I began my journey as his prophet, and I'll end it as his host."

Merrill's smile only widens, and Abel flinches back from the sheer madness that lurks there. It's almost like Merrill is catatonic and speaking on autopilot.

"We've spent enough time here hiding and crawling underground. Fresh air and virgin wilderness awaits. We're off to claim a mountain."

Merrill chuckles, his hand reaching out to companionably slap Abel across the cheek. Abel feels his heart sinking. He feels the dark pressing in, and he fears that there is no light left to stop it.

118

"No rest for the wicked, Ivy."

She rouses herself from a swampy, half-remembered dream, and she's back in the stinking muck of Fort Armistead. Merrill looms over her, and he's busying himself by removing her chains and lifting her up to a vertical base. She tries to launch herself at him, jaws snapping together, but Merrill easily plants a forearm against her chest and holds her back.

"Play nice. I hope you've got your traveling shoes on, because we've got miles yet to go."

"What did you do to Abel, you sick fuck? I heard the screams."

"I taught Abel how to stop being a liar. I helped him to be honest. It wasn't hard. He's naturally a pretty submissive individual."

"And you've always liked that, haven't you? For people to submit to you. Trust you blindly and do what you want them to do. Such a good little manipulator."

"I hate when we quarrel, Ivy. You never submitted to me. Your will has always been iron. I'd break my teeth if I tried to bite through it."

"Before this is over, I'll break your teeth myself."

Merrill smiles and lowers his head, gently taking her by the arm and leading her through the catacombs. She notices that the place is eerily quiet now, no sounds to indicate that the Coyotes are still camping down here.

"I assume you got what you wanted?"

"For now."

"What's the endgame? You can't just keep us imprisoned forever. Braun is going to realize what you've done. You might have been able to handle three wolves with your deranged mortals backing you up, but what if he sends a much larger group? They'll shred through your ranks, Merrill. You know that in your heart."

"I do. I've never been the biggest or the strongest, Ivy. I flex what's in my skull more than any other muscle. I realize that time is of the essence. They will come, but when they do, it'll be too late. I will have a god in me."

They emerge from a little slit doorway that exits the underground bunker, and they begin to make their way through a section of scraggly woods. The trees open up ahead and Ivy sees the open water of the Chesapeake Bay lapping at a trash-lined shore. There's a small parking lot, all cracked asphalt and broken streetlamps, and the RVs and beater vehicles that the Coyotes travel in are sitting here, almost waiting for the cue to depart the premises.

Merrill begins to lead her to his personal RV, and she shakes him off and turns to face him head-on.

"Do you plan to kill us?"

He looks genuinely hurt, almost incredulous that she'd even think of such a thing.

"You think me capable of that? I don't kill things that I love. And a part of me still loves you, Ivy. It's why your scent has stayed with me for so very long. I just can't let you go. Wolves mate for life, after all."

He leans in, and he smooths down some of Ivy's clothing, wiping bits of dirt and mud from her cheeks.

"You're a messy girl, but we'll clean you up. We'll make a queen of you. Even a god needs a queen. We'll sit in the clouds of Mount Lykaion, and I'll let you suck the blood of our enemies off my fingertips. I'll feed you, fuck you, and give you a world that is raw and meaty. A kingdom befitting carnivores. And in return, you'll give me sons and daughters. You'll carry our little titans in your womb."

He presses a hand against her stomach, a wistful sigh escaping his lips. Ivy can barely hold back her shock and disgust.

"You boast about how mighty your brain is, but I can see it in your words, Merrill. You've gone rotten. You're not clever. You are completely fucking *insane*."

"And you're tired, Ivy. You're tired and you're dirty and you need a wash. We'll speak again when you're less inclined to use your tongue like a knife to cut me with."

He takes hold of the back of her head and plants an intimate kiss on her forehead, a few strings of saliva spreading out as he pulls back. She repays his kiss with a quick snap of her neck and a headbutt that catches him right on the mouth, splitting his bottom lip and causing a little stream of blood to flow freely down his chin. He responds with a grin, reaching up with his thumb to rub the blood around his mouth, tasting of his own life force. Harvey Hollow comes up behind them and takes hold of Ivy's arms, and Merrill nods in the direction of the RV door.

"Be gentle with my future bride, Harvey. She is a spitfire, and I wouldn't want her any other way!"

Ivy is forced up the steps into the stuffy little RV, and then the door closes behind her, shutting out that brief bit of sunlight she was allowed to feel on her skin.

"I thought you'd want to ride with Ivy."

Abel is sitting on a cushion in the dingy confines of one of the RVs while Merrill is in the kitchenette area making a pot of black coffee.

"She's upset."

"Hm. Being held against her will and watching one of her closest friends get slaughtered might have something to do with that."

An oppressive silence lingers, nothing but the sound of the RV rattling as it navigates the road ringing in Abel's ears. Merrill's back is turned to him, and it appears that he's using the claw on his index finger to stir the coffee.

"Seems she did a number on your lip."

"Wounds heal, Abel. Some faster than others. She'll come around."

He turns and takes a seat across from Abel, bringing the mug up to his lips and sipping from it. He winces a bit when the hot liquid passes across the cut, but the flesh is already starting to stitch itself back together. The perks of being a wolf: the healing factor is next-level.

"What happens when you find your mountain?"

"Revelry. Carnality. A ritual must be built up like a fire. It takes stoking. The circumstances have to be just right to make it work. And you'll have a prominent place in the festivities, old friend."

Abel feels anxiety crawling under his skin, and he doesn't like that little mad twinkle in Merrill's eyes.

"What might that entail?"

Merrill leans forward, grinning as he sips his coffee. He uses his thumb to trace the rim, almost drawing out the suspense. It's like he can smell Abel's frayed nerves, and he relishes the scent.

"It's a surprise."

"I'm not a big fan of surprises, Merrill."

"I'm not a big fan of interlopers nosing into my business at the worst possible moment, but here we are. Intertwined fates. There's poetry in that."

Abel lifts up his hands and scrubs at his grizzled facial features. The manacles jingle, and he rubs his fingertips across his throat and chin, noticing that the silver-inflicted lacerations there are starting to close up. It takes longer for the healing ability to kick in if silver was used to create the wound.

"Let's imagine for a moment that everything you believe about Apollo Lykaios is true. This ritual plays out the way you want it to, and you summon a divine essence into your body.

The world becomes yours to play with as you see fit. What then? You destroy mankind? You wipe out mortals because you hate them that much?"

Merrill's eyes widen, and a belly laugh bursts out from him, shaking the big man's body and making him tremble. He even slaps down a hand across the table while trying to get a grip on his mirth.

"You think I hate human beings, Abel? You've pegged me wrong. I don't have some grand fantasy of killing the world and ruling over cinders. No, silly goose. I'm humanity's reminder. I'm going to break the cities and tear apart the tapestries of refined civilization. I'm going to let the wild creep in again. Nature only needs the slightest push to retake what it has lost. The trees and the vines and the thorns will choke out the remnants of buildings and vehicles, and new growth will sprout up and reach valiantly for the sun."

He sips his coffee, eyes flickering over to the window and the view of the forest that they're driving past.

"And as for the people? The billions and billions of people that call this planet home. They'll shed their suits, their careers, and their material possessions. They'll be reminded of their animalism. That long-buried instinct that exists inside of every man, woman, and child. I'll reach my claws down into the core of the human species, and I'll encourage them to devolve. They'll live in the forests again. They'll hunt, they'll eat, and they'll fuck like rabbits. They'll walk with wolves and they'll learn from wolves, and for those worthy, when the time is right, they will become wolves."

Merrill points up to the front of the RV where several cannibals sit together, a few of them munching on bones and dozing in the sunlight that filters in through the windshield.

"That's the future of humanity, Abel. That's what happens when you rip off the polished veneer of societal expectations.

People revert to their bestial nature. It's freeing for them. They remember that they have teeth, and they're taught how to tear with them again. That's what I want for this world."

He leans back and runs his hands through his hair, smoothing it along the base of his neck.

"I want for people to remember that they have always been animals, and in the end, it is *okay* to be an animal. Not just okay. It is fucking *glorious* to be an animal."

Abel has gotten to the point where he knows it's folly to try to reason with this man, but what else can he do in the face of such a tirade?

"Society exists for a reason. Rules, structure, and restraint. If that falls, there is only havoc, Merrill. Why can't you see that?"

"Because it's a safe view of the world, and it's terribly narrow. We'll have to agree to disagree."

Merrill rises up to his feet, the floor beneath his boots creaking under his weight. He moves to the other section of the RV with a little sliding door, patting Abel on the shoulder as he goes.

"I'm in the mood for a power nap. Entertain yourself for awhile, but don't do anything too strenuous. There's great work on the horizon. Closer than you know."

The door to the small bedroom slides closed, and Abel is left to his own thoughts, none of which are comforting.

CHAPTER 17

Ivy sits and she broods. She lets her eyelids flutter closed, shutting out the RV and drifting into a safe mental space where no one can disturb her, not even that creep Harvey Hollow who sits in the corner using a toothpick to clean his filed teeth.

She realizes that she volunteered for this. It felt like a moral obligation at the time because of her old ties to Merrill, but now she sees that it was a terrible mistake to come at him with peacemaking in mind. He's a war dog now, and conflict is all he understands. There's no trace of that boy she used to know. He was timid, thoughtful, and had a real capacity for compassion at times. That boy would never force her to be some queen to a demagogue, but she has to stop thinking of

Merrill in that context. When she looks at him, she still sees a ghost of the past, and it's time to let that die. If there's even a sliver of that boy left inside of Merrill, it is withering and dying inside of him, choking to death on ego and fanaticism.

She has to make a plan. It feels like everything that has happened in such a short time has been like a whirlwind, and she hasn't even had time to properly think. The cannibals attacking, the death of Pyke, and then being drugged and carted from one side of the country to the other—it was bound to leave her feeling drained, and maybe that's exactly what Merrill wanted.

Her body is exhausted, her appetite hasn't been properly satiated, and even the wolf within is weary. Her heart is heavy and she has not had the chance to mourn. It feels like one big nightmare, but she only needs to open her eyes and look at Harvey to confirm that this is reality, and there's no escaping it unless she acts. No more sitting back and accepting this. It's time she found her fangs again.

"Tell me something, Harv. What's it like playing human beta to an alpha wolf? You gnaw on the scraps he doesn't eat? You let him piss on you to mark you as his toady? Something like that?"

Her eyes open, and she stares daggers into the chief Coyote. He smirks, leaning forward while swishing the toothpick back and forth in his mouth.

"It's an honor. We are the chosen few, and we'll sit at the head of his table on Mount Lykaion."

"I see that you've got a taste for his Kool-Aid, and I bet you've guzzled gallons of it. The truth is that he doesn't give two shits about you, Harv. He sent you to fight his battle for him like the yellowbelly coward that he is. A mortal against a wolf is suicide, but somehow you managed to kill Pyke, so I'll give you kudos for that. You have balls. It's a real shame to see them twisted up in a rubber band, just waiting for Merrill to snip them and castrate you. You're just a meat shield to him, man. It's fucking *sad.*"

Ivy shakes her head, leaning back against the cushion of the seat and placing both hands casually behind her head. She baits the hook just a little more, her smile as taunting as it gets.

"You're not really fit to be a wolf, ya know. I picture you more as a scavenger nipping at a wolf's tail as it feeds. Begging for remnants of a carcass, the paltriest strings of gristle. Simpering and mewling and hoping. Harv the Hyena. That's you in a nutshell."

Hollow's face is reddening, and it's clear that Ivy is under his skin. He goes over to one of the cabinets and digs through until his hand lands on a meat cleaver with a pitted blade. He retrieves this, brandishing it before Ivy and running his thumb along the dull, ragged edge.

"Wolves heal so fast, and I've always admired that. Merrill wants you intact, but I don't think he'll mind if I carve a few steaks off your hip first, Ivy. The skin will grow back. I think I'll cook some of you on that stove over there, and then I'll eat those steaks while you watch and feed you a few medium-rare pieces of yourself."

"Aw, Harv. Don't threaten me with a good time! Show, don't tell. Let's see what that little cleaver can do."

Hollow exhales deeply through his nose, lowering his shoulders and making a beeline for Ivy. He lifts up his arm and swings the cleaver, aiming for her exposed leg, but Ivy shifts to the side and thrusts her hands upward, and the blade connects with the manacles binding her wrists together. There's a horrible clang of metal meeting metal, and then one of the manacles on Ivy's right wrist breaks completely, the silver mechanism shattered. She darts up to her feet and piefaces Harvey, shoving him back with all of her strength, and he tumbles head over heels down the aisle in the direction of the bathroom.

Ivy doesn't bother following, instead she heads to the cab of the RV, and she half-transforms as she goes. Her left wrist is still handcuffed, so she allows that portion of her body to remain human, while one side is all wolfen and wild, chestnut fur, claws like sharp porcelain, and teeth dribbling with saliva.

She thrusts down a paw and drives her clawed thumb into the driver's ear, rupturing his eardrum and making him scream, and then she leans down and simply bites off half the man's head, crunching through skull and slurping down a big gray slab of brain. He sits there convulsing for a moment, hands still gripping the wheel, and the big RV is careening to the side without proper guidance. Ivy rips the man out of the seat like a broken flesh doll, his body smacking up against the windshield and leaving spiderweb cracks smeared in red, but before she's able to grip the wheel and get the RV back on the road, one tire flips down a little roadside gulley and the whole vehicle is rotating, spinning on its axis and flipping Ivy around inside like an astronaut with no gravity. She hears Harvey grunting somewhere in the back while trying to hold onto something, and then there is the sound of glass breaking, metal shrieking, and trees snapping as the RV flips over itself multiple times.

Despite the unexpected violence, Ivy enjoys the ride.

CHAPTER 18

Harvey punches up through a ventilation shaft, the hatch popping off, and then he yanks his body up through the hole, his bloody teeth gritted and a small gash oozing from his temple. The RV flipped over itself numerous times before crashing against some tall elms at the edge of the forest, and it's nothing but twisted metal and a smoking engine now, the windshield shattered completely. He flops down onto the ground and pulls himself to his feet, spitting out a glob of blood and snarling to himself at the audacity of that little she-bitch to pull something like this on him.

"What in the *fuck* is this?"

Merrill is stomping down the hillside from the road, the Coyotes trailing behind him in small groups. The entire caravan of vehicles has stopped and pulled over to the embankment to check on the crash.

"She went rabid, my lobo. She chomped on the driver before I was able to get her under control."

Merrill glares out into the woods, and he sees absolutely no sign of Ivy. The big man unleashes with a blood-curdling roar, and his hand morphs into a paw that he uses to claw at the side of the RV in a fit of rage, leaving deep lacerations in the roof. It takes him several moments of heavy breathing before he's able to calm down, and then he turns back to Harvey with more of his composure intact.

"Where are we?"

"Last I checked on the GPS, we had just passed the state line into West Virginia."

This seems to improve Merrill's mood just a bit, the mad wolf nodding to himself and appreciating the splendor of the wilderness that surrounds the road.

"The Mountain State, and peaks on every horizon. That's good. It's fitting that fate brought us to Appalachia, and it's Appalachia where a new Mount Lykaion will be christened. You're with me, Harvey. We leave the vehicles behind, and we hoof it into the bush from here. Our mountain is waiting."

Merrill turns back to the cannibals surrounding him and he motions The Chemist forward. The man is eager to oblige, shambling forward and presenting his melted face to his master.

"Put together a hunting party, and scour these woods until you find her. Her scent is close, and she hasn't gotten far. Do not kill her. Take her alive and then follow our tracks. We'll reconvene in the valleys beyond."

"As you wish, Mister Sade."

A frail cannibal next to The Chemist speaks up, the little urchin digging at pressure sores along his torso. He looks diseased, a runt of the litter.

"What if she's gone too far?"

Merrill spins around, places his entire palm around the cannibal's face, and draws him intimately close. He pulls his terrified body in until only one eye is peaking through Merrill's splayed fingers.

"You find her even if she's traveled to another *fucking* dimension, and if you do not, I will eat you, digest you, and shit you out into your mother's mouth. And rest assured, I'll track your mother down to do this for the pure spite of it. Are we crystal?"

The cannibal struggles to breathe through his nose, nodding emphatically while in Merrill's squeezing grip. Sade lets the man go and pushes him away, and then he climbs atop the side of the smoking RV and makes his voice loud and proud for his followers.

"My brethren! Come to me like settlers on the frontier. Walk with me into the great wilderness. This is Appalachia, and it's here that we howl and we roar and we throw our combined voices into the wind. There's an old god waiting in those blasted hills, eyes like embers in the coal mines, teeth big enough to carve ravines, and if you want to meet him, you need only follow in my footsteps."

There are barks and excited screams and shouts of merriment, and with the Coyotes firmly in his pocket, Merrill leaps down from the RV and leads the way into the forest, Harvey falling into step beside him.

The Chemist breaks away with a group of his own men and women, and they head north instead, following a fresh trail of broken branches and marred soil. The she-wolf is out there, and they must find her.

CHAPTER 19

Ivy doesn't waste time thinking, she just runs. Her long coltish legs leap over rotting logs and tapestries of thorn, and she lets the carpet of moss underfoot cushion each stride. There's a little blood dripping down from a cut along her cheek, but it's superficial, and it was worth it to wiggle her way out of the RV's ruined windshield after the crash. She's managed to put some distance between herself and the road, but she knows it's only a matter of time before Merrill sends his hounds after her.

This forest is thick, and it provides good cover. If she's forced to make a stand out here, she likes her chances, but not unless she's able to fully transform. After what seems like an eternity of sprinting, she slows her speed and comes to a full stop near a few large boulders. She gazes down at the one manacle left on her wrist, and she's satisfied to see that it was damaged in the crash. There's some bruising along her forearm, and the metal along the cuff is warped. It's still holding, but it looks like with some proper motivation, she can finally get the damn thing off.

She moves over to the closest boulder, sucks in air, and slams the cuff up against rock. There's a shockwave that travels up the bone of her arm, but she can take it, and she won't be deterred. She repeats the gesture, and this time there's a clunk noise as the cuff hits rock, and a piece of the mechanism fails. Her fingers reach down, momentarily steaming as she grazes them against the silver spikes, and she violently rips the cuff from her wrist and tosses it down to the ground.

A savage smile spreads across Ivy's face as she flexes her now-free hand and stomps down on the ruined cuff, grinding her heel against it and burying it into the loamy soil. Now the wolf is uncaged, and the beast can birth itself whenever she pleases. Good news for her, bad news for Merrill and his ilk.

Merrill trudges through the foliage, his head lowered and his thoughts burning through his mind. Harvey is in close proximity, and Abel is being led by a chain connected to his manacled wrists, with several of the cannibals hauling him along when he stumbles or slows down.

He has mixed feelings about being in Appalachia. Just one state over is the place that rejected him, and a small part of Merkel Valley will always exist in the shadowed chambers of his heart. It is coated in black sludge, and most of the teachings that he learned there have been purged from him. It's too painful to hold tight to dead memories. There is only the road ahead, and the destiny that he knows is his to claim by canine and claw.

He's thinking of Ivy. His hand reaches up, and he brushes against his lip. There are a few flakes of dried blood there, and he rubs those off, but otherwise the wound has closed up and healed completely. She can't be far, and he hopes he hasn't made a mistake by putting his confidence in The Chemist. She's a piece of his past that he never thought he'd see again, and now that she has reemerged into his life, he sees that she was always meant to have a place at his side. It hurts to think that there's a newfound hate in her, and it's like she doesn't recognize him anymore. He's been cold and he's been cruel, and there are blades of guilt in his guts for insinuating that she'll be his queen whether she wants to or not, but he wants her to want that as much as he does. His life has been a string of rejections and abandonments from those who were supposed to be his closest allies, and he's tired of letting those insults stand. There's been a gaping hole in his soul for so long, and although his Coyotes help to fill it, he knows that the only thing that'll close up that internal pit for good is the essence of Apollo Lykaios.

The god of the wild understands his rage and his pain. Apollo has been cut off and imprisoned too, and like calls to like. Two lost souls being drawn together, and isn't there purity in a beautiful kinship between outsiders?

Merrill claws past ferns and thick vines, the elevation changing as the hills climb higher, and in the distance he sees a towering green peak on the horizon. There's majesty in the mountain, and for just a moment, his breath catches in his throat. Something clicks in his head, and he knows.

He catches Harvey by the shoulder, and he points forward, directing his lieutenant's gaze forward.

"There."

Merrill nods, conviction filling him up.

"That's where we're going."

He walks faster now, and his cannibals pick up their pace to keep up with their master. There's no time to waste.

Mount Lykaion is eager to receive them.

CHAPTER 20

The Chemist leads his men and women deeper into the woods, and he notices that it's gotten darker. The tree line above is thick, and it chokes out sunlight, allowing only a few enterprising rays to pass through the tangled branches. The Coyotes at his back are armed with knives and hatchets, and he carries a machete that's been dipped in molten silver, giving it the appearance of a half-melted sword. It's a fitting weapon because it matches his half-melted face.

He moves slow and with purpose, each step quiet, and he knows they're on the right track. There was blood spatter on the leaves further back, and Ivy's tracks have led them into a boulder maze. Giant mossy hunks of rock, claustrophobic passages, and trees that have grown up and around the boulders, roots splayed across them like stone snakes. He has the Heretic's Fork in his satchel, and if they can subdue her long enough to get it onto her neck, then she won't be able to put up much of a fight at all. But he's banking on those silver manacles still being on her wrists. That's the difference between hunting handicapped prey and coming face to face with bloodthirsty death.

He stops, noting a smeared red handprint on the side of one of the boulders, and he motions two of the cannibals forward. A woman with stringy blonde hair and pallid skin, and a man with a foul beard and bloodshot eyes. The Chemist points with his machete, and they round a corner ahead of him, checking for any sign of the she-wolf.

He waits, crouched down with the rest, and he hears a quiet skirmish. It isn't loud or horrific, but it's the silence of it that scares him more. There is the noise of clothing and flesh parting, liquid hitting the ground, and then a muffled cry of anguish. A severed leg comes flying out from around the corner, the boot gone, crusty toenails pointing up in the direction of the sky. It was severed at the upper thigh, and The Chemist can't tell if it belongs to the man or the woman.

He knows fear intimately. Fear came to him once in a little aluminum trailer where chemicals blew up into his face, turning his skin to roaring fire, but this is somehow worse. This is the terror of the unseen, and he will not let it stand.

"Go and get the bitch, and cut her to the marrow. Leave her leaking, and you make damn sure you don't let up until we've got this collar secured on her neck!"

His little pack of cannibals bursts forth ahead of him, and he follows. There's no sign of the two scouts he sent except for a hot pile of organs sitting in the middle of a tight passage. He can make out a pancreas, three lungs, and the broken remnants of stomach with a partially digested peanut butter and jelly sandwich spilling out of it.

And then, like a lightning strike, she's there, and she attacks from above. She's loping across the boulders above them, and her paw swipes down and cleanly carves through a man's head, splitting through skull and puncturing brain. He drops, and she appears again, her head smashing through vines and leaves as she clamps her teeth into a woman's shoulder and pulls her up into the foliage. There's a wretched gnawing sound, and then the woman's body is thrown and crushed against a rock on the opposite side.

Ivy flips herself down in front of them, all raging wolf, and she towers above the cannibals. She's mowing through The Chemist's hunting party, splitting open bodies and chewing through musculature, and no knife or hatchet that finds her deals anything but the most superficial damage.

The Chemist panics, and he thinks for a moment of running, but Merrill would pick his bones clean if he did that. Instead he remembers his insurance policy, and he reaches into the inner folds of his jacket and takes hold of it. Ivy is a foot away from him now, and she has a large man by the throat, her paw crushing his windpipe as she chews a gaping crater into his chest. Her enormous teeth crunch through ribcage, and she swallows his lungs before letting him drop. She wipes her mouth, and then she lunges for The Chemist.

She takes hold of him, and he can feel her hot animal breath blasting in his face, and it reminds him of that evening in the trailer. The burn. That blistering burn, and perhaps it's always been his destiny to face it. The entire course of his life has been a painful swim through flames, so why not embrace it?

Her jaws open wide, and he sees row after row of hooked fangs that have the ability to turn his skin into mincemeat. His eyes close, and he whispers to her before the first bite can come.

"If you live, tell Merrill I'll be watching from hell as he takes our god into himself, and I'll be cheering."

Ivy pauses, not understanding, and then she lowers her snout and looks downward. The Chemist can't smile properly due to the scar tissue of his twisted mouth, but he gives it his all. And then he pulls the grenade from the inner folds of his jacket, holds it at chest level between them, and pulls the pin.

There's a percussive explosion, and a blast of seared meat and smoky blood follows. His body flies backward, a deflated balloon, and Ivy is blown backward as well, her spine smacking up against one of the boulders. Both combatants fall into the dead leaves of the little clearing in the boulder maze, and there is nothing to be heard but the after-silence of the grenade.

And then, when the critters of the forest feel that it's safe to resume, birdsong begins anew.

Ivy awakens coughing up smoke, and she feels like she just slept in a barbecue pit. She reverted to her human form after being knocked out from the grenade blast, and she has to crane her neck down to survey the damage. Her clothing is charred, and there are superficial burns on her flesh, but they're starting to heal. The tissue is most damaged near her sternum, where there's a little hunk of shrapnel, and with a trembling hand she reaches up and yanks it free. It didn't go in deep, only about two inches, but that's enough to cause a little spurt of blood to bubble out once it's removed. If she had been mortal, the explosion surely would have ruined her. She has the lupine DNA to thank for her survival.

She rolls to her side, and there isn't much left of The Chemist to see. His body was devastated by the grenade, his chest a gaping crater, one of his arms blown clean off, and his face just blackened meat with a few cinders floating up from it. He's as dead as dead can be, and she's grateful for that. Before she went down, she was able to dispatch the entire hunting party, and that means for now, she isn't being pursued.

She flops back down to the ground for a moment and just takes the time to breathe and rest. Her eyes flit across the clouds, the endless peaceful blue, and she wonders if there's something up there that's laughing at the brutality that's going on down here on planet Earth.

Merrill is beyond redemption. His actions fill her up with revulsion, and just the thought of him makes her angry. This was cemented when he crowed about her being some unwilling queen to a god, and how she wished she could have taken out his jugular at that moment instead of only crushing her head into his mouth.

There's no time to wait and hope for Braun to bring reinforcements. If she were to go back to Merkel Valley and raise up an army of wolves, it would be too late by the time they'd tracked Merrill down. She's the one that has his scent, and she believes the responsibility is on her. He's close now, and she knows that she won't have a hard time finding him. If she can secure Abel's freedom, that's two wolves, and more of a fighting chance.

She's done being hunted.

It's time to do the hunting.

CHAPTER 22

Merrill smiles as he climbs, hands reaching down to graze through mountain laurel, his nose full of honeysuckle and deep earth and the best combination of forest scents. He can feel a low vibration under his feet, like this mountain has waited, volcanic and timeless, seeking an interdimensional eruption. He trudges under hemlock, spruce, and pine, relishing the burn in his calf muscles and the excited hoots and hollers from the cannibals at his back. This feels right. This feels like hell hiding beneath Heaven. It must happen here. There's no question, he has found his Mount Lykaion.

They're closing in on the summit, and it's a lush clearing, a woodland meadow that must have been logged at some point in the distant past. The wildflowers are so thick that you could lie on them and sleep on nature's mattress, and the clearing is alive with bees, birds, and squirrels leaping from tree to tree.

Merrill pauses, and he closes his eyes. His nostrils flare, and he simply lets all the conflicting smells assault him. In this moment, connected to the thrumming fibers of the planet, he absolutely loves being a wolf. He knows in his heart that he was always meant to be such a thing, and it was always fated for him to open the door to legendary fangs and a bloodlust that has been denied for far too long. He briefly forgets about Ivy. He forgets about Merkel Valley and whatever retaliation they might have brewing. He is in the forest, and this is the sort of place that would never deny him, shun him, or cast him out like a leper. This is the wild, and it welcomes the wounded. He is home.

For a moment, a storm passes over his features. He glares over his shoulder, seeing the Coyotes lurking there, the stinking mass of them, all carrion-eating urchins that he has gathered from the darkest corners of the country. He sees Hollow with his aviators and his scarred arms, a wolf-slaying freak, and isn't it strange that Merrill should find himself in the company of wolf-slayers?

There's a chance here, and it won't be here forever. He could turn his back on the summoning. He could disband the Coyotes and send them off into the obscurity he plucked them from. He could deafen his ears to Apollo Lykaios, and he could accept that the old beast god was exiled from this world for a reason.

But most of all, he could let Ivy go.

He reaches down, and he plucks a trillium flower up and into his palm. He caresses the white petals, appreciating the purity of the little wild, growing thing. The flower reminds him of Ivy.

They had love once a long time ago. He remembers looking into her eyes and seeing everything he ever wanted. His ear to her chest, her heart thumping so loud and proud, and he would have liked to have listened to that sound for eternity. It was young, foolish love, and perhaps that is the best kind. Life hasn't had a chance to tarnish you, to take from you, and you can just be in that moment and taste of that love. He can taste it still in the far back of his throat. It is sweet and floral, like trillium.

So yes, he could let her go, and in doing so, he could let the past go. He could let the old hurts heal. Merrill thinks on this, probably one of the most important decisions of his lycanthropic life.

And as he thinks, he remembers his hate. The way it boils in him, burns through him, makes the wolf within feel infected with rabies, frothing at the mouth, eyes bleeding, heart howling, claws rending at his insides in an effort to have some small amount of comfort. He hates that he hates, and that makes him hate more. Merkel Valley never wanted him. Braun never wanted him. His biological parents never wanted him. Ivy has proven that even she never wanted him.

Merrill Sade remembers his hate on the summit of Mount Lykaion, and he forgets to forgive. He turns to his cannibals, brow twisted, teeth gritted, and he balls his fist around that trillium. The petals are ruined, their fragility lost, and he drops it to the dirt where it can stay.

"I want bonfires that reach as high as the moon. I want a banquet that is red and raw and merciless. And I want all of you to fuck and kill and turn this meadow into a place for animals. Night comes, and with it, a god. Reach into yourselves, and give me the worst of yourselves. Apollo Lykaios is coming—"

Merrill starts ripping at his shirt, letting his hands turn to claws, shedding that garment along with whatever remains of his humanity.

"—and I am his door."

The cannibals pour forth on either side of him in hordes, fighting each other, dancing with each other, ripping the clothes off of each other, and giving in to debauchery. There is only a little daylight left, and it is dying.

It won't be the only thing that dies here.

Abel kneels in the night, and he watches the birth of a hellscape. Fires dominate the mountain summit, giant dead tree trunks fueling them, and the cinders float up into the sky to mingle with the stars. The cannibals are a blight upon morality, and it seems they've waited for this moment since joining Merrill. The chance to forsake all shame and sensibility, and it's like witnessing the devolution of the human species. They slow dance with each other around the bonfires, drunk on moonlight and perversion. They mutilate each other with their little knives, kissing and cutting, hands smearing blood against trembling lips, the realms of pain and pleasure seeming to melt together into some hedonistic mockery of Eden. There is bestial sex, the men taking the women in the open, smashing their faces into the dirt, scrubbing their skin against pebbles and rocks, handfuls of hair balled tight into angry fists. The women bite and tear with fingernails, lusting for desecration, and some of them take hatchets to the cocks of their mates, carving new holes there, and they explore those holes with their tongues.

Blood splashes across mountain laurel, tainting the petals, making filth where there was once beauty. Abel watches as a man with scabs on his brow begins to tear his own entrails out of his abdominal cavity, and once they're free and the loops drag in the soil, he collapses down into a fetal position with a sick grin plastered on his face. There seems to be some kind of pecking order, only a select few of the Coyotes handpicked for self-mutilation and murder. It's like they know they're the chosen victims, and they relish the honor of being rendered into broken and tattered meat.

There is a banquet that lords over this nightmare waltz, and that is what seems to be the focal point here. The eating of raw and living flesh, eaters and the eaten embracing and loving one another, content with their roles, and somehow doomed to play out this performance in servitude to Merrill. A rudimentary dining table was constructed of logs and bark, and it's here where the feast takes place. Body parts decorate the table: organs, dismembered limbs, and partially cooked genitalia. Coyotes sit naked on the logs, their bodies as unclothed as when they were born, and they glut themselves on the carnivore buffet that's in front of them. Many of them stuff themselves so full that they are forced to vomit, spewing up torrents of glistening eyeball, colon bits, and small shards of rib. It takes everything Abel has for him to keep from becoming violently ill just watching this.

He distracts himself by glaring up at Merrill. He's above the table, perched on an outcrop of cliff that overlooks the clearing. Harvey Hollow is with him, and in Hollow's hands is a black satin pillow with the broken remnants of the crown laid out neatly atop it.

Merrill has cultivated this inhuman animalism, this orgy of rot and ruin, and now he's doing the last thing that's left to do. He's assembling that scorned headpiece.

Abel feels the power of it even from his place on the outer rim of the madness. It's a dark current, like ozone crackling, something just itching to cross over.

This is a little pocket of the purest chaos ever orchestrated, a Sacrament of the vilest carnality, and it is now or it is never. This is Abel's worst fear.

This is the environment where Apollo Lykaios thrives.

CHAPTER 24

She lopes on all fours, her human form abandoned for the moment, because time is of the essence. Leaves and thorns smack her snout, her tongue lolls, and her golden eyes are orbs that cut through the vastness of the night. The insects sing and the frogs chirp, and the forest breathes, and Ivy breathes with it. Deep inhalations that fill up the lungs in her canine chest, and even from miles away, she can see the bonfires on the summit of the mountain.

She can smell cooking flesh—almost pork, but not quite. She can hear shrieks and screams and merrymaking that celebrate all things vile. Her paws dig furrows into the earth each time they make an impact, her powerful hip muscles working overtime to keep her going at optimum speed. She's a wolf possessed, and she knows exactly what is waiting for her up on that mountaintop, but she races for it anyway.

She can hear it, smell it, and sense it.

It's hell.

When the cannibals come for him, Abel doesn't resist. He is pulled through smoke, cinders, and pandemonium. The world around him is red. If it is not the great fires licking at the sky and forming strange shapes there, it is blood, everything drenched in blood. The wildflowers are soaked, the grass is full of droplets, and more is being spilled all the time. Humans have given up any semblance of being humans on this mountaintop. They've tapped into some eldritch compulsion to self-destruct and go feral. Merrill has made beasts of these people without ever even having to turn them. He has reached into the hearts of these outcasts and brought out the darkest emotions lurking there.

Abel is dragged forward, and he trips over severed limbs, flaps of flayed skin, and teeth pulled from gums like speckled pebbles. From all sides of him, there are vague shapes in the smoke and the firelight—the Coyotes acting out their nameless ritual—and the chewing is almost musical. That is the sound that dominates Mount Lykaion now.

Ragged, needy *chewing.*

He stumbles past a naked woman with greasy white hair laid out on the earth, and crouched near her lower half are two shadowed figures. They are in the process of stripping meat from her legs and eating the strips raw, and she seems to be in a kind of religious rapture, almost oblivious to her own defilement. She catches Abel by the pants leg and scratches her fingernails teasingly against his ankle. Her eyes are red-rimmed and crying mucus. She smiles up at him, and blood bubbles coat her incisors.

"It's nice, isn't it? I feel it in my sinew. Something is coming from another place. Something aches to be born. . ."

Abel stares down at her, swallowing his own fear and disgust, and then his jailers keep him moving. He is yanked and pushed until he's finally on that same rock outcropping that overlooks the clearing, and there is Merrill, arms wide, twitching in and out of his human and wolf forms like a fanatic who has lost all control. Merrill throws his arms open: fingernails, claws, fingernails, and then claws again.

"Didn't I tell you that you had a purpose? You've always been special, Abel. You're wanted. You're needed. Let me validate you. Give yourself to something greater than yourself, because that's selfless, and that's kind. You're my martyr. Come here now, and let me see you."

The cannibals toss the manacled Abel into Merrill's open arms, and Merrill catches him by the face. He runs those hands across Abel's cheeks, letting the tips of the claws trace little indentations into the skin. Abel can barely stand to look at Merrill now. The corruption in him seems to seep from his pores, and he smells of spoiled meat and mutilated sanity.

Merrill throws his head back, and he roars up at the sky, spittle flying from his lips. He sounds furious, his anger boiling up from a nowhere-place deep inside him.

"He is my own kind. Flesh of my flesh, full of fang and fur and instinct. We are brethren. But I give him to you, oh Father of Ferals, Lord of the Untethered Wild. I open him for you. I gift him to you. Let his innards oil the hinges that open up the door, and see what I sacrifice for your freedom."

Merrill's nostrils flare, and his jaws are elongating, tongue a lashing spear behind his teeth. Abel stares him down, and he shows no fear.

"I forgive you, Merrill. You can't help what you are."

The words are drowned out in snarls, barks, and howls of rage. Slobber pours from Merrill's blackened lips, and he grinds his teeth, giving voice to all that consumes him.

"For you, Apollo Lykaios, I eat my own."

Merrill then snaps his neck forward and takes a huge bite out of Abel's face, crunching on nose, orbital sockets, and jaw. Abel staggers, his features a pouring crater, eyes and nose a broken faucet, but Merrill pulls him close, and he keeps on biting. He holds him in his arms like a lover, and he bites his face off under moonbeams, licking scalp, munching ears, pulverizing skull with canines, and through it all, Abel's body goes into a violent seizure while still vertical. Merrill keeps chowing down on his face until there's nothing left there but a ragged stump of a neck, and he swallows down meaty chunks of head, belching and shaking his own shaggy head from side to side, seeming drunk on the cannibalized flesh of a fellow wolf.

He flings the decapitated body off the rock outcrop, and it falls like a rag doll before splattering onto the ramshackle dining table. The cannibals descend on the scraps, fighting over those warm morsels of lycanthrope meat.

Merrill is swooning, and he remains in lupine form, his mouth a wide grin of gristle and euphoria. He drags his own claws against his cheeks, cutting through fur and flesh, a tortured lament causing him to succumb to something like derangement. He turns his grin of gristle onto Harvey, and he eyeballs the crown with a hunger that is cavernous.

"My body is his house, and it's time to invite him in."

Merrill spits out Abel's glasses, the frames warped beyond all hope of repair. He drops to a knee, kneeling and lowering his head like he's ready to be knighted.

"Crown me."

180

Ivy bursts free from the foliage into the clearing just in time to see Abel's headless body, thrown from above, splat down into the chaos of the cannibal's feast. She freezes in place, a tremor passing through her entire form, and then a blood-curdling howl of lament breaks from her lips. It's like emotional catharsis, and Merrill hears it from his perch above the festivities, his attention moving from Harvey and the crown to her emergence at the tree line.

He roars down to her, his eyes just malevolent lamps shining in the dark.

"There she is! You're late for the last supper, but I assure you, there is enough of Abel to go around. Don't mourn. His meat goes to hungry bellies, but his essence lives on in me."

She doesn't waste time with more insane words. She brings the wolf to the forefront, and she blazes into the clearing, but immediately she's met with a wall of stinking blood-smeared bodies, cannibals dogpiling her and striking out at her with fists and filed teeth, and she fights hard, shredding the majority of them, but their combined weight is taking a toll. She has her teeth buried in a Coyote's throat, his tough jugular spouting into her mouth like a faucet, and that is when she notices the enormity of their weight lessening atop her. She hears growls and ripping sounds from above. Ivy is finally able to shove her way up through the limbs, and the sight that greets her is enough to strengthen her resolve.

Reinforcements have arrived. Wolves from Merkel Valley are running and leaping atop cannibals on all sides of her, snarls and lacerating claws making music on the mountaintop. It's a beautiful cacophony, and she sees Braun there in his human form, a bearded sentinel, and before she knows it, his hand reaches down and takes up her paw, pulling her to her feet so that she can join the fight.

It's happening so fast, and there's no time to take a breath or rest. She must hunt until the hunt is done, and Mother Moon shines hard on her wounded heart. Her kin have come, and she is restored.

War spills across Mount Lykaion, and Ivy wades into it.

Merrill sees them pouring into his sacred place from the rock outcrop, and the rage feels like acid in his veins. They're usually pacifists, but tonight they've chosen violence. The ghost of Merkel Valley haunts him still, and he snarls seeing Braun down there, the big man strolling through his Coyotes and snapping necks while still in human form.

"Give it to me, Harvey Hollow."

He motions for the crown, and Harvey is quick to deliver it into his master's hands. Merrill locks eyes with his trusted soldier, and he snaps his chin in the direction of Braun in the clearing below.

"Protect me. He can't interfere. We've come too far to let them take this from us."

"With my life, my lobo."

Harvey stares at Merrill, the wolf who saved him from a broken life of senseless pain, and he pulls a pair of silver brass knuckles from his belt. He removes his shirt, exposing self-harm scars, and he begins to work his way down the cliffside.

He scoots halfway down granite on his backside, and he finds himself across the killing field from Braun. The old alpha of Merkel Valley changes in front of him, turning wolfen, all rippling muscle, razor-tipped claws, and thick gray fur that sprouts lush from his ears.

Harvey Hollow is mortal, and he knows without armor, this is likely a kamikaze mission. But he is a Coyote, and Coyotes know no fear. He steels himself, and he moves forward.

Braun swipes at him, paw heavy with murderous intent, and Hollow ducks the blow and peppers the werewolf in the ribs with a shot from the silver brass knuckles. Braun grunts, thrown off balance, and he grabs onto Hollow, mauling him with claws, but Harvey smashes a headbutt into his hairy chest to gain separation. Hollow wipes the blood from the shallow cuts on his sternum and he leaps onto Braun's back, biting down into the muscular shoulder with his filed fangs, but Braun catches him and flips him over his shoulder.

Harvey smashes down into the dust, and he assesses the damage his body has undertaken. His wrist is broken, several of his ribs are shattered, and there's a laceration near his navel that goes deeper than the others. But even so, he pulls himself back to his feet, and he turns to face Braun.

He defiantly spits his own blood up and splatters the old werewolf in the face, and he runs at him, rearing back with his good wrist in an effort to smash the silver knuckles into the lycanthrope's jaw, but before he can close the distance, Braun sidesteps and cleanly whips his claws through Harvey's flesh, cutting his throat and chopping through his windpipe. Hollow coughs violently, blood pouring down across his chest, and he locks his hand around his throat. He stumbles and falls back into the smoke, and somewhere where visibility is low, he falls.

Braun brings up a balled paw, and he smacks it against his chest while gazing up at Merrill. The message is clear.

Your death comes next.

CHAPTER 26

Merrill watches Braun make quick work of Harvey, and his lips pull back from his teeth, his canines snapping together in frustration. Smoke forms a halo above his head, wolf ears twitching, and he eyeballs the crown in his hands. It hums, a low vibration, and it's hot to the touch.

He casts his gaze skyward, and he sees ripples in the firmament, a place where reality is thin and a threshold begs to be crossed. With something bordering on reverence, he lifts the crown, and he allows it to settle onto his skull. The stone pulses, and it sends shockwaves through his head, little torpedoes of eldritch energy. He roars, and he opens the door.

"I wear the Crown of Carrion, and I summon thee. . ."

The sky splits above his head, and the stars cleave themselves open. Merrill sees enormous amber eyes, and they are the size of the moon. He sees fangs that are joined together, mashed against each other, rolling maws of canine and incisor, mouth inlaid with mouth. There is a tongue that stretches the length of rivers, and it lashes from within the maw, showering the killing field in drops of cosmic saliva. The sky howls into the hellscape, and the sound is so powerful that it makes the earth beneath his feet shake. Fur, muscle, and raw sinew. The Father of Ferals. The ultimate animal. He is all teeth and terror and an ancestral song that makes rabies burn in the blood.

He stinks of dog pens and forest floors, and Merrill feels the crown melting against his head, becoming a part of him. Bloodlust of an incalculable weight settles against his soul. His eyes turn a blistering amber, and they begin to bleed rabies-infected plasma. His teeth sharpen, shoving and pushing against each other, making of his mouth a pit of knives. He grows, musculature splitting his skin, fur becoming a giant black mane that tapers out along his back.

He growls and snarls and howls and screams, and it is agony to be a god. It is the purest fucking pain ever conceived, and Merrill welcomes it. He throws his arms wide, jagged railroad spike talons bursting from fingers, forearms, and elbows.

He doesn't bother to climb down from the cliff. He leaps, his gigantic mutated body landing with a crash, and this landing craters the soil and splits the very bedrock underneath. Merrill takes his first steps, and he walks through the fires, clawed feet stomping through burning logs.

He does not catch aflame. A god does not burn. The outside can't burn when his insides are already on fire. A low, vicious growl broods in the far back of Merrill's throat, and he tramples through infernos to meet Braun head-on. He feels the essence of Apollo Lykaios licking his brain and chewing on his thoughts. He feels the old wolf god running in circles through his heart, craving blood and flesh and subjugation.

Braun is watching him, his former alpha clearly unnerved not just by what Merrill has become, but by the sheer self-destructive madness of even allowing such an unstable entity into this realm of existence.

When Merrill speaks, a hot, sour wind travels through the trees, and rivers of white froth pour down from his slavering lips.

"Are you proud of me, old man? Look upon me. See me before I swallow your eyes. Not your black sheep, but your black wolf. And rest assured, my heart is blacker now than the root cellars you locked me in when I misbehaved. When I acted against your will."

"You've damned yourself. That thing inside you will rip you apart at the seams. No man or wolf can endure it. It will burn you out. I tried to protect you from it, Merrill. I did everything in my power to make you stay away. You needed to be taught. You needed discipline."

Merrill grins, and his laughter booms through the clearing, cannibals and werewolves fighting to the death on all sides of them.

"I needed your love. I needed someone to give a fuck. But I was never one of you. Always on the outside looking in. The bad one. The wrong one. I thought that about myself for years, and it tore me up inside."

Merrill lifts a tree-trunk-sized arm, and he looks at the glistening talons that have emerged from it. He flexes his hand, and there's nothing but raw, thrumming power in the digits.

"So I think it's only fair that I tear apart your insides. Let's feel it together tonight, Braun. It'll be a bonding experience."

Braun transforms to his full lupine form, a formidable alpha, and he roars at Merrill even though he is dwarfed in size. He races forward, claws and teeth ready to slice, but Merrill meets his charge. Merrill butchers the only father figure he ever had in a matter of seconds. It's not even a fight, it's an immediate slaughter. When Merrill barrels into Braun, it's like the old alpha goes into a wood chipper. His body explodes into red mist and chunks of brutalized viscera. Merrill basks beneath the exploded carcass, and he catches the spinal cord in his fist, whipping it around his head wildly. He unrolls his tongue like a hideous carpet, and he lets the plasma droplets collect on it. His former father figure tastes like torments that are never forgotten, and what bliss that taste is.

Meat. Meat. Meat.

Merrill thinks only of *meat*, and Braun is not enough.

Apollo Lykaios crawls around inside of him and pisses on his heart and his spirit, marking territory, and the old wolf god howls for more.

Ivy's snout is awash in blood, her teeth sore from tearing, and it takes everything in her not to curl up into the fetal position on the ground when she sees Merrill shred Braun into chunky pieces. A wave of hopelessness hits, and she gets a closer look at what Merrill has become. A gargantuan, hulking Goliath that seems invulnerable to damage, and Merkel Valley wolves are charging him from all sides, leaping to attack, but he swats them away like small gnats, their torn bodies flying off above the tree line.

A raving cannibal runs at Ivy and slashes at her with a silver knife, and she ducks and buries her face into his side, chewing at the ribs and mauling the man with her claws. She throws him behind her shoulder with her teeth and makes a beeline for Merrill, having to wade through bodies and skirmishes to close the distance.

A wolf called Mallory blazes forward to her left, cutting off a Coyote that was trying to sneak up on Ivy from behind, and she clamps her jaws around the unfortunate urchin's ankle and begins to drag him across the ground. Mallory, who has light blonde fur, is a newer arrival to Merkel Valley along with her husband: they've proven themselves to be invaluable to the homestead on numerous occasions. Good people, and even better wolves.

Ivy nods in appreciation, using her paw to swipe blood from her eyes, her chestnut fur slicked back with hot steaming plasma, and she focuses on Merrill once again. He's mowing through Merkel Valley residents like they're absolutely nothing, and if his rampage continues, he and his Coyotes will kill every single wolf that she has ever had the pleasure of knowing. She has to end him. She has to find a way.

She becomes aware of a presence beside her, and she turns, seeing Mallory's mate next to her. His name is Asher, and his thick brown fur is coated in blood too, the remnants of his kills smeared across his eyes and snout like warpaint. She doesn't know him well, he'd only been in their company for about a year before Ivy departed to hunt Merrill, but in that brief time he established himself as a wolf to be remembered. A quiet soul, but a strong soul. Braun helped him to come to terms with the animal inside, and he was eager to learn. She can see in Asher's eyes that he wants vengeance for their fallen leader as much as she does.

He points an onyx-colored claw in Merrill's direction, and Ivy sees that he's motioning to the crown that's almost welded into Merrill's head. It seems almost to be acting as hub, some blasphemous artifact that is allowing him to channel and control the power of Apollo Lykaios.

"We take him together."

She growls in agreement, and then Asher jets into the smoke, his hind legs tearing up dirt as he goes. Two Coyotes try to stop him, and he shoulders through them, smashing their frail bodies to either side to clear a path. Merrill's back is turned as he lifts a wolf and bites their head clean off, tilting the furry body up and drinking from the neck like a bottle of liquor. He turns just as Asher races at him, and he smashes down a giant foot, Asher just barely manages to dodge it and avoid being crushed into paste. The much-smaller wolf leaps and scrambles up onto Merrill's hip, and he uses it as a pivot point, propelling himself higher into a wild leap, and with Merrill's enormous rotating jaws snapping the air, only centimeters from cutting him in half, Asher connects with a clean impact, his right paw smashing the crown and his claws digging through the stone.

It splits from Merrill's head, tearing off scraps of his scalp and his hair as it goes, and it tumbles down to the ground, and before it can be touched by any sycophantic Coyote, Asher takes it up in his jaws and runs as far from Merrill as he possibly can.

The wolf god clamps his paws against his enormous pulsing skull, and he roars until his vocal cords bleed.

When the crown falls from his head, Merrill feels like he's imploding. That raw, feral power is sucked out like a vacuum, and the influence of Apollo Lykaios goes with it. The last he hears of his demigod is an enraged scream inside his head, and then his body is deflating, limbs sagging downward, the skin stretched to inhuman proportions, impossible even for his lycanthrope physiology to bear. He shrivels, muscles contorting painfully, and he spits up a foul-smelling black bile from deep within his sternum. He spins on his heels, desperate to retrieve the crown, but Asher has vanished into the smoke and the melee, and Merrill's knees feel so blown out and wobbly that he doesn't think he could pursue him even if he tried. He is reduced to his human form, a violated and mutilated version of his human form, the body warped and reshaped by containing an essence so much more powerful than itself. He shambles forward, squinting through the thick black plumes, and that is when Ivy tackles him to the ground like a wolfen torpedo.

His spine cracks against the earth, and he feels ribs break inside of him, made brittle by his becoming. She assumes her human form while straddling him. Wild chestnut hair, face drenched in the blood of his cannibals, and teeth gritted together as she breathes out her rage with each exhalation.

They lock eyes. Merrill's black irises are glazed, his face drooping against his skull, the skin ruptured and the texture deformed. Ivy's features are a cauldron of emotion, so much aggression, pain, and sorrow flowing through her veins.

He looks up at the she-wolf, and then he lets his gaze drift around him, taking in the full view of the killing field. The tattered chunks of meat that used to be Braun, the headless body of Abel plastered half-eaten on a dining table, and wolf and cannibal bodies lying scattered across the wildflowers, their blood soaking into the mountaintop.

His voice is a croak, barely audible in a broken whisper.

"For once in my life, I wanted to be something special. Someone big. Someone powerful. I wanted to be a god, because I thought a god would never feel alone."

Merrill coughs, and the emotion in his voice is genuine, choked with blood and dripping with regret. His attention keeps flitting across the damage he is responsible for tonight, almost like he's seeing it for the first time with new eyes. His gaze looks hollow, strangely lost.

"I think I went about it the wrong way."

Ivy realizes that she's weeping, the tears cutting little paths through the blood-caked pores of her cheeks. She can't tell if the tears are born from rage, hate, pity, or lost love. Deep inside, she thinks it's a mixture of everything, and before another word can be said, she thrusts her hand downward and smashes her claw-tipped fingers through Merrill's chest. She sinks herself into him up to the forearm, and he watches her while she does it. His eyes are glassy, and they're far away. Her fingers twist past veins and soft organs, and she takes a firm grip of that warm beating thing that's in his center. She holds his heart literally as she once held it figuratively. Her lips tremble, and she tries to think of parting words, but there are no words. What's done is done, and this is all that's left. They both seem to understand that on an unspoken and instinctual level.

Instead of speaking, Ivy gives voice to a howl, throwing back her head, plasma droplets flying from the tips of her hair, and she rips Merrill Sade's heart from the open crater in his chest. She squeezes it, draining the aorta, ruining the ventricles, and pulverizing the flaws and the mistakes and the bad choices that festered in Merkel Valley's wayward son.

He dies quietly and without fanfare, an expression of resigned acceptance settling over his features. He dies a husk with nothing of a god left within him. His body relaxes, and in the end, he doesn't look fearsome. He looks lonely.

She lifts her head, teeth gritted, heart-blood pouring down her wrist and dripping off the point of her elbow. She holds it up high, and she lets the Coyotes see. There are not many survivors, most of them mauled and murdered by wolves, but those that are left are shocked to see their master dead and in the dust. They do not remain. They run and scatter into the trees, fleeing for the woods.

They respect only power and domination, and in that moment, with a wolf heart in her hands, Ivy is the alpha.

CHAPTER 28

Once the war is won, Ivy takes time to rest. She wraps Merrill's heart up in a torn cloth from her shirt, and she carries it with her as a totem. Her fellow wolves are busy collecting their dead and loading them onto a carriage that was brought out from the brush, and she watches as woolen blankets are draped over the ones who lost their lives on Mount Lykaion. Seven lycanthropes slain, Braun and Abel among them. There are dozens of deceased cannibals in comparison, most of them mauled and torn to bits, and Ivy is fine with letting their bodies lie. They can be food for the vultures, and she thinks it fitting that scavengers feed other scavengers.

Asher and Mallory approach her, the couple arm in arm, looking weathered and blood-stained, but alive. Ivy wouldn't have made it without them, and her confidence in the fledging wolves has been bolstered even more. They belong in Merkel Valley. They've earned their fangs and their fur.

"What of the crown?

Asher tilts his head behind him, looking beyond the clearing and deeper into the woods. The huge bonfires that the Coyotes built are dying down, and only a few cinders remain in blackened pits all around them.

"There's a cave not terribly far. Lots of passages and a stream deep inside. I chewed up the stone with my teeth, and I spit the pieces into the mineral water. Nearly broke my canines doing it, but now it's finished."

She nods, swallowing deeply. She trusts Asher, and she knows in a forgotten place like that, whatever is left of the crown can languish in the dark forever.

Asher turns and looks at the shriveled cadaver that used to be Merrill, his jaw tightening as he examines the remains.

"What should we do with the body?"

Ivy looks around, the cannibals split and torn here and there, already starting to attract flies. She won't have him buried in the homestead. It would be a cruelty to plant him in the same dirt as Abel and Braun. He chose to be a wolf apart, and that decision will have to follow him into the wilderness beyond.

"Leave him with his followers. He'll return to nature. It's more than he deserves to become one with the forest floor, but it's the best thing. He couldn't grow as a man, but maybe beautiful things will grow from his carcass. That's all there is."

Asher and Mallory remain solemn, and it's clear they don't have an alternative suggestion. All three of them look to the horizon, and they see burning yellow sunlight emerging from behind distant peaks. After lasting darkness, Ivy almost chokes up and cries to see even a hint of dawn. That light signifies a lot for her. Rebirth, endurance, and the chance to start anew. Merkel Valley needs that. *She* needs that.

Her emotions feel raw, her spirit scraped and gutted. She wants to dive into a river and rest her back on the bottom, letting the pebbles grate against her skin while the water washes her clean. Without Braun, things will be different. The homestead will need guidance and stability. It'll be hardscrabble, but Ivy wouldn't want it any other way.

She gets a firmer grip on the cloth-covered heart, and there is catharsis. Much like the wolves themselves, the past transforms, becoming different, stronger, and more capable.

Time is a werewolf, and the future longs to howl.

CHAPTER 29

Many hours pass, and the denizens of Merkel Valley vacate the mountaintop, taking their dead with them and leaving nothing but ash, gore, and new blossoming rot. The vultures arrive, and they make a dinner of soft eyes and ears. The opossums crawl down from branches, bringing their offspring with them, and they eat delicate strips of skin from opened bodies. A buck wanders through around evening, his antlers mighty, and he lets his hooves slam down across the corpses, a small show of disrespect for those that dared to control and tether Mother Nature. She is a fickle woman, and these fools learned that the hardest way of all.

Twilight fades, birdsong retreats, and a VIP guest arrives at the clearing. It is huge, cratered, and casts out an ethereal glow, painting the mutilated Coyotes in a sour shade of canary yellow. It is the moon, and it is full tonight, gown open and roundness gleaming.

Moonbeams fall on the pitiful thing that used to be Merrill, and for just a moment, his shoulders twitch, his body trembles from side to side, and it appears that a resurrection is nigh. But there's no life in Merrill's eyes. He is the king of husks now, and nothing more than that.

His body moves because something has taken hold of the ankles, and that something has stretched its jaws wide to take Merrill's feet into a cavernous mouth that drips with frothy slime. There are crunching noises, and a meaty slurping. The mouth gapes, and it moves up Merrill's body centimeter by centimeter, akin to an anaconda slowly feasting on a particularly coveted meal. It takes almost the entire night to eat him all, but in the end, every last scrap of Merrill Sade is consumed and digested.

There is the sound of bones twisting, muscles contorting, and that awful, hideous mewling that comes with a first transformation. But this is a reverse transformation, the eater returning to his lesser form, and there comes a satisfied gurgling from deep in his guts.

He trudges across those that he once called brethren. He scents the air, and he finds it sweet. He hears things that he has never heard before. And they're not the chattering nightmare voices telling him to carve himself up with kitchen knives. It's different this time. These sounds are woodland sounds, loud in his eardrums, and each one is like a little song.

He wanders in the wilderness, because in his heart, he has always been a wanderer. It takes time, but his nose doesn't betray. It leads him to a different mouth entirely, the wide open mouth of a cave, and each droplet of cavern water from the upper stalactites is a siren telling him come hither, and so he does. The bats flutter and retreat, and even the cave crickets hide their spindly bodies from him. They sense that something is wrong with him, and they avoid being infected with whatever that something is.

He begins to whistle, and it echoes back to him, making goosebumps break out across the twisted scar tissue that adorns his arms and his upper chest.

A little stream glistens in the far back of the cave, the water crystal clear, and the eater plunges his gnarled hands down among the isopods and the salamanders that make a home of the frigid water. He reaches deeply into the slick pebbles, and he comes up with a different kind of stone entirely. Broken shards of a crown, sigils still warm to the touch, and the aroma of burnt fur creeping off of it to tease his nostrils. The magic in the crown is shattered, but the world is full of magic, and he prides himself in traveling alongside broken and unwanted things until the time comes for a fix.

His reflection is in the mineral water, and he smiles with filed fangs even while in human form. Cracked aviator sunglasses. Flesh a map of self-mutilations. A new white scar across his slashed throat, barely healed, the mark of his unintentional making.

Harvey Hollow rubs a hand across his belly, feeling the meat of Merrill settling there, and it's the most special feeling of all.

"Sleep inside of me, old friend. I'll need your strength."

He inhales deeply, and the broken bits of crown arouse his most forbidden and bestial appetite.

"I am the lobo now."

One Year Later

The valley is alive with fireflies, and the children run and catch them on the tips of their fingers, marveling at the living light contained within. A warm breeze travels through Merkel Valley, and the homestead feels like the sanctuary it was always meant to be. There's a tribunal tonight, and it's the first in a long while. The elders are gathered, those wise old wolves, and the communal campfire blazes high, the aroma of charcoal and honeysuckle dancing through many sets of lupine nostrils.

Ivy sits atop a chair of intertwined antlers, heavy ancestral wolf pelts draped across her shoulders. Her hair is braided with crow feathers, polished canines, and petals of wolfsbane. Dark, smoky makeup adorns her eyes, and her gaze is locked on the firelight, reflecting the controlled chaos of the flames. The wolf inside of her paces, and she does her best to calm her nerves. Asher and Mallory sit on a log near her, arms around each other, basking in the warmth. Asher's beard is long and braided with bits of rawhide, and Mallory has a new pink hook-shaped scar along her temple. It only adds to her natural beauty. Their teenage daughter Cara stands behind them, and Ivy sees so much of Mallory in the young woman's features.

Asher grins, nodding silently, and Ivy swallows and grins back. The elders wear heavy woolen cloaks, and their gnarled hands beckon to her.

"What do you give up for Merkel Valley, Ivy Faeworth?"

Her hands reach into her lap, and she finds that her fingers tremble. She begins to peel back the tattered cloth, and Merrill's mummified heart becomes visible. It is dried like leather, and it carries the vaguest perfume of spice. A single tear cuts through the smoky makeup to roll down her cheek and catch against her lip. She tastes it there, hot and salty, and it brings a sort of brittle closure. There's a naïve little girl buried deep inside of her that wants to hold onto that heart just a little longer, but the woman she has become knows better.

She looks to the elders, and her gaze is steel.

"Everything."

Ivy casts the heart into the fire, and it crackles as it burns, sending little whirling embers up into the night to mingle with the fireflies. It acts as a catalyst. Wolves begin to transform all around her, their shaggy heads thrown back as they howl out their support for her. A summer celebration, and Merkel Valley's lycanthropes welcome it with fang and ferocity.

"Rise then. Rise as our alpha. She who protects. She who leads. She who guides the great hunt under the glow of Mother Moon."

Ivy rises, and she walks barefoot across the coals, her eyes yellow lanterns in the dark, her fangs gnashing, and she falls into the embrace of her kin. There are hugs, kisses on the cheeks and forehead, and a general sense that she has made it back to the one place in this world that has always been sacred to her.

Asher and Mallory hug her tightest of all, the quiet wolf whispering into her ear that he can't think of a better lycan to lead them.

There is food, drink, and dancing. She takes it all in and speaks with her kin, promising better days ahead, and it warms her soul to know that she will do everything in her power to deliver on that promise.

When there is a lull in the festivities and people have splintered off into little groups to talk, Ivy takes the chance to be alone for awhile. She strolls past the campfire and beyond the cabins, and she pauses at the graves of Braun and Abel, the mounds grown over with big thatches of lush purple wolfsbane. She kisses her fingertips and throws it down to them, letting herself briefly travel to the land of memory.

Her respects paid, she keeps moving, the soil feeling good beneath her bare feet. Wet grass tickles her ankles, and she inhales the forest, scenting hemlock, acorn, and the moss that carpets their cabin rooftops. A brood of cicadas emerged a few weeks ago, and they're everywhere in the trees now, their melody humming and rising from the branches, and it reminds her of a tidal wave lapping in and out. She appreciates their music, and the longer she listens, the more it seems to heal.

She touches the cracked brown husks that they emerged from, thousands of them dotting the trunks of towering spruce trees that drip with sap. It took time, but she's shedding her husk too, and her wings feel wet and new. The old wounds on her flesh healed quickly, as they are prone to do. There are deeper wounds in her soul, and even the lupine gift can't heal those overnight. She has to sit with them, trace claws across them, and one day, those internal scars will be stories.

Ivy will heal because she has to. She'll fight her battles silently, and she'll come out on the other side and run with the beams of Mother Moon.

It's the alpha thing to do.

THE END

ACKNOWLEDGMENTS

The end of the story has come, as all ends do, and I'd like to express gratitude to those that helped make Crown of Carrion the book that you now hold in your hands. I want to thank Ravven White for taking a chance on Crown and opening the publishing house for this one. I sent Ravven the manuscript to beta read quite awhile back, and I was so pleasantly surprised when she offered to give this one a home (along with another novella of mine called Soulmates).

I've talked shop with Ravven twice now in person at big horror writer events in Philadelphia and Richmond, and I deeply admire how she believes in her authors & champions the books that are under the Corvid umbrella. It means a great deal to count myself as one of those authors now.

Huge shout out to my editor Maddy (maddys_needful_reads) for helping me to define my voice in this one & polish it into a much better book. I'd also like to thank Grace R. Reynolds and Stephanie Kemler for all the long conversations about writing, inspiration, and this crazy imagination-fueled dark fiction sphere that we all exist in. I've known Grace and Stephanie for years now, and both of them are also published by Curious Corvid (Grace is a modern day

Shirley Jackson and Stephanie is the Philly vamp queen, so please check out their work as well, it will speak for itself) They always told me such positive stories about having books released through Curious Corvid, so it felt like a purely natural fit for me to join the Corvid crew as well.

Thank you to the Word Weavers for accepting my depraved brain demons, and thank you to my readers for sticking with me. It's been a few years since my last novella, and I feel so motivated to create new tales heading into the future.

I wrote Crown of Carrion in 2021 during a tough period in my life, and I wasn't sure if it would ever find the right home. It is a fully standalone book, but it's set in the same universe as an older novel of mine (Old Hollow) so fans of that book will get to see some closure for a few of the characters they met many years ago. Although my werewolves are supernatural beasts, they're also painfully human. They have flaws, doubts, and abandonment issues. Merrill Sade is the most flawed and complex of them all, and I hope that translates. He searches for meaning in the all the wrong places, and he pays for it. But while Merrill loses himself, Ivy finds herself and perseveres, and I think that message of hope shines through.

Well, my claws are tired of tapping the keyboard, so for now, I'll say farewell. Think of me the next time you see

Mother Moon, and never be afraid to show the world your fangs.

ABOUT THE AUTHOR

Jeremy Megargee has always loved dark fiction. He cut his teeth on R.L Stine's Goosebumps series as a child and a fascination with Stephen King, Jack London, Algernon Blackwood, and many others followed later in life. Jeremy weaves his tales of personal horror from Martinsburg, West Virginia with his cat Lazarus acting as his muse/familiar. He is a native of Appalachia and you can often find him peddling his dark words in various mountain hollers deep within the wilderness.

Soulmates

A novella by Jeremy Megargee

When two lost souls connect via cyberspace, they bond over their shared inner darkness. Together they explore each other's mental illness' and phobias, pushing one another into dangerous and depraved acts of devotion. What started as a longing for connection twists into a downward spiral of perversion and toxicity splattered in blood and lust. Their final act begs the question: how far are is one willing to go to feel loved?

www.ingramcontent.com/pod-product-compliance
Lightning Source LLC
Chambersburg PA
CBHW060444310726
48977CB00001B/314